CON-fidence

CON-fidence

TODD STRASSER

SCHOLASTIC INC.

New York Toronto London Auckland Sydney
Mexico City New Delhi Hong Kong Buenos Aires

ISBN 0-439-57949-X

12 11 10 9 8 7 6 5 4 3 2 1   3 4 5 6 7 8/0

Printed in the U.S.A.   40

First Scholastic printing, October 2003

To Regina, John, Kate, and the crew at Holiday House,
thanks for letting me do this.

chapter One

Lunchtime in the cafeteria. In your hands is the sandwich your mom packed. Two pieces of yellow American cheese between two plain white slices of Wonder Bread. You gaze off across the noisy room, ripe with the scent of sour milk and the sickly sweet odor of rotting apple cores. Kids squeeze together at tables and devour their lunches. Pressed so closely their elbows are pinned to their sides, sitting like rows of squirrels, chattering and laughing, happy to be with their friends.

You are not happy, nor are you sitting where you want to be.

The center of the cafeteria is Krista Rice's realm. Her table is jammed so tightly with girls that, if one of them sneezed, the wanna-bes at the ends would fall off their seats and tumble to the floor. Queen Krista sits in the middle of these girls. She is small and dainty with straight dark brown hair, big brown eyes, a cute upturned nose, and a light sprinkle of freckles. She is certainly one of the prettiest girls in your grade, but there is something extra about her that the other pretty girls don't have. It's a sheen that radiates from her hair, eyes, and lips, from her clothes. It is the glow of confidence. The special knowledge that every other girl in the grade secretly wishes she were her. Krista is the ultimate "Don't-You-Wish-You-Were-Me" girl.

"Stop it, Lauren." Your best friend, Tara Snead, places her plump elbows on the lunch table and leans forward.

A warm flush crosses your face. "What?"

"Don't pretend you don't know." Tara points a black-nailed finger toward the middle of the cafeteria. "You were staring at Krista again."

You look down and take a bite of the cheese sandwich your mom packed. The girls at the Don't-You-Wish-You-Were-Me table buy school lunches. They wouldn't be caught dead bringing a wrinkled brown paper bag from home. Hunger is a powerful sensation, especially here on the outskirts of the cafeteria. Out here at an almost empty table near the door with the red exit sign above it. Out here where a cold draft wafts in from the hall and there is elbowroom to spare. You could stretch out along the seats and take a nap if you wanted. Here in the realm of the socially inferior.

You chew slowly on your plain-tasting sandwich the way your mind chews slowly over every thought. Oddly enough, Krista Rice was once your best friend. Back in grade school. Back before she moved to a nicer neighbor-hood and became snotty and backstabbing and boy crazy. Back before she turned on you.

And you turned to Tara, a chubby raven-haired girl with a pretty face and black fingernails. All soft corners except her sharp tongue. She writes poems about death, and brings three teriyaki beef jerkies from home every day. She always finishes the first two quickly, then slowly savors the third, as if painfully aware that it will be her last nourishment until the school day ends.

"Who's the new girl?" she asks.

You swivel around and look across the cafeteria. A girl you've never seen before has just come out of the lunch line carrying a tray. She is tall and pretty, with a petite nose and straight blond hair that hangs down to the tops of her shoulders. Wispy bangs cover her fore-head and fall into her eyes. She is wearing jeans and a light blue turtleneck sweater. Holding the tray, she looks around and her half-hidden eyes seem to fix on the DYWYWM table where Queen Krista holds court.

Strangely, the DYWYWM table has gone quiet. The A-list girls pause from their gab and gossip to study this new arrival. The rest of the kids in the cafeteria carry on with their normal everyday jabber, but you hardly notice. Instead, you are acutely aware of the silent spot in the center of the otherwise noisy universe.

The new girl turns to an empty table near the

windows and sits by herself. The girls at the DYWYWM table start to chatter once more. You gaze a moment longer at the new girl. Through the windows the red, yellow, and orange leaves drop from tree branches and float lazily to the ground. It is mid October—a strange time of year for someone to start school.

"She looks like a sheepdog with that hair in her eyes," Tara observes. "How can she see?"

"Same way a sheepdog does," you answer.

Tara chews sullenly on her last jerky. "I think we're going to hate her."

"Why?"

"Oh, *come on,* Lauren." Tara has no patience when you pretend to act dumb. "You *know* why. Just look at her. She's pretty and has nice clothes. Unless she's a total spaz, she'll be sitting with Krista by Christmas."

"Looks aren't everything," you reply, and take another bite of your utterly uninteresting sandwich.

Tara pinches her nostrils with her fingertips and speaks in a nasal voice: "Yes, Mrs. Walsh."

Your name is Lauren Walsh, and *Mrs. Walsh* is your mom. And Tara is right. What you just said is exactly what your mother would say.

And she would be severely wrong.

Because here, at Woodville Middle School, with very few exceptions, looks mean just about everything.

two

"You happen to be very pretty, Lauren." Mom stands behind you at the little white makeup table in your room. You sit, looking at yourself in the small mirror outlined with smoky white bulbs. Is she telling the truth? She's your mother. She'd probably say you were pretty even if you had a wart the size of a golf ball in the middle of your forehead. She lifts your hair, giving it some bounce and body. "You just have to do a little more with your hair."

"I'm plain."

"You're not plain. You're fair skinned and pale. Why don't you try a little makeup?"

Only the DYWYM girls wear makeup. If you tried that, someone at school would be sure to notice. They'd snigger and say you were trying to be an A-list girl. It's safer not to try.

The new girl's name is Celeste Van Warner. She has what teachers call "a lively personality and a winning smile." She wears eye shadow and lip gloss and can always think of something clever to say. By the first week of November,

Tara's prediction has come true. Celeste has a regular seat at the DYWYWM table.

But Celeste isn't entirely like Krista and her snotty friends. Where Krista will never begin a conversation with anyone who isn't "A-list," Celeste seems nice to everyone. You and she have gym and math together, and you have seen her chat and laugh with girls who Krista Rice wouldn't be caught dead speaking to.

Lunch in the land of the socially inferior. Today your mother has packed sliced turkey on whole wheat. Through the windows, the few leaves that remain on the trees have turned brown and wrinkled. Most have fallen to the ground.

"Want to go to the mall after school and Christmas shop?" Tara asks. "Lauren? Are you staring again? Yoo-hoo, Earth to Lauren."

You look back at her. "The weirdest thing just happened."

"Krista choked to death on a meatball?" Tara guesses hopefully.

"You wish."

"No, Lauren. *You* wish."

"That girl, Celeste, just smiled at me."

Tara makes her eyes wide with pretend disbelief. *"No!"*

"I'm serious."

"Seriously psycho."

"Why do you always have to be sarcastic?"

Tara sticks out her tongue at you. "It's my defense mechanism. So she smiled at you. What's the big deal?"

"It was a *nice* smile. I mean, she's sitting with Krista, but she still acts nice."

"So?"

You can't explain it. Tara's too sarcastic and defensive. It's a shame because she really does have a pretty face, but she's heavy, and sometimes the other girls say mean things about her behind her back. And not *so* far behind her back that she is completely unaware. Tara knows what they say. She's decided that she will never be popular, and now she doesn't even try. In fact, she goes out of her way to make them think she doesn't care.

But you were once Krista Rice's best friend.

And why you aren't sitting at the DYWYWM table right now is the greatest mystery of your life.

chapter
three

"You have to stand up and defend yourself when they pick on you."

"I know, Mom, but it's hard."

"What does Tara do when they pick on her?"

"They don't dare. She's too quick. They know if they cut her down, she'll come right back with something even nastier. But I'm not like that. I can never think of what to say."

In math you settle down at your desk and open your book. When you look up, Stephanie Eisley is standing over you.

Stephanie is a skinny girl with long streaked blond hair. Her eyes are too little and her mouth is too big. She sits with the wanna-bes at the end of the DYWYWM table and would be the first to fall off if someone sneezed. You've heard that the only reason she gets to sit at the table at all is that her father owns Carmen's, the nicest restaurant in town. Twice a year he lets her have a pizza party there with a deejay, and all the pizza and soda anyone could ever want.

Now, looming over you, Stephanie has a cruel smirk on her oversize lips. The room has gone quiet. You don't have to look around to know that everyone is watching.

"Hey, Lauren," she says, "I hear your mom's so fat there's a sign on her back that says, 'To be continued.'"

Your mom isn't fat. But it doesn't matter. Around the room, kids chuckle. Stephanie waits to see if you'll reply. You've heard a million comebacks, but suddenly your mind is as blank as the chalkboard.

"Your mom's so dumb she took half an hour to cook minute rice." Stephanie hits you with another one.

You freeze in panicked terror, afraid that whatever you say will come out wrong and the other kids will laugh even more. But out of the corner of your eye you see Celeste, two rows over. Her eyes are hidden behind those bangs; her lips are pressed into a hard, flat line. She is not smiling.

"Your mom's so ugly they tried to put a paper bag on her *shadow!*" goes Stephanie.

Tears start to well up in your eyes. *Oh, no!* You blink hard to force them back.

Mr. Youngstrom, your math teacher, comes in. "Seats, everyone."

Stephanie returns to her desk. With brimming eyes,

you stare straight ahead, not daring to move or blink for fear that giant tears will spill down your cheeks.

Mr. Youngstrom starts to write on the board. You wait as long as you can, and then dab the tears away with the cuff of your shirt. At the same time you carefully glance around. They're all watching Mr. Youngstrom. *Except* Celeste, who is watching *you*. Feeling embarrassed, you quickly yank your sleeve away from your face. But Celeste does not wrinkle her nose or sneer. Instead she purses her lips in a sympathetic way, and nods as if she understands.

You can't wait for school to end. Still feeling the raw burn of Stephanie's cut downs, you want to get away as fast as you possibly can. At the end of the day, you pause at your locker to grab your jacket.

"Hi," a voice says behind you. You turn. It's Celeste.

"Oh, hi." You nervously brush a few strands of hair off your face. Celeste parts her blond bangs with her fingers as if to get a better look. Her eyes are grayish green.

"Hair." She rolls those eyes as if it's a big pain.

"Yeah." You roll yours.

You both giggle.

"Don't let Stephanie get to you," Celeste says. "She's a jerk. Severely insecure."

"I guess." Feel the color rise on your cheeks. You don't know Celeste. This could be a trap. You must be careful about what you say, lest Celeste goes running back to Stephanie to tell her.

But Celeste changes the subject. "You really understand that stuff about equivalent fractions?"

"Well . . . yeah."

"Wish I did. I don't know whether it's me or Mr. Youngstrom. But I'm just not getting it."

The pace in the hall quickens as kids hurry to their buses. "I could help you."

"Really?" Celeste asks.

"Sure." This is like one of those medieval torture racks that stretch people in two directions at once. You have to get to your bus, but how can you leave this A-lister who's acting so friendly?

"Maybe you should give me your number," you suggest. "I could call you later."

"I wish." Celeste sighs. "Our phone's been all messed up ever since we moved. The phone company keeps coming back to fix it, but they never get it right. It's such a pain."

Two kids run past you, their backpacks bouncing behind their shoulders. "I really have to go."

"Catch your bus?" Celeste realizes. "Why didn't you tell me? Come on, girl."

You both start to run. Ahead through the doors you see the last kids climbing onto the buses.

"You can come to my house now if you want," you offer at a gallop.

"Cool."

You're out the doors and running for the bus, both of you laughing for no reason. It all happens so quickly. Celeste Van Warner is coming to your house!

four

You and Celeste sit together on the creaky, squeaky bus. You're feeling queasy, but it's not motion sickness. The brief thrill of her coming to your house has turned to dread. This could still be some kind of trick, although with every passing second it seems less likely. Celeste's friendliness feels genuine. But what will she think when she sees the little one-story houses in your neighborhood? Most have yards no bigger than throw rugs. Even the trees, with their skinny, dark branches, seem small. You've ridden your bike through Hillside, the neighborhood where Krista and some of the other DYWYWM girls live in large two-story houses, some with three-car garages and lawns big enough to play touch football.

"You mustn't think that way," you imagine your mother saying. *"Having more money doesn't make anyone better than you."* Judy Knight and Rob Carlucci both live near you in little houses like yours, and they're A-listers. And Sean Evans, whose father owns a company that builds malls, is mean and conceited and despised. But

the girls whose parents have more money wear nicer clothes and throw nicer parties. Some of their parents go away together for summer vacations. Having more money doesn't automatically put anyone on the A-list, but it doesn't hurt, either.

You and Celeste get off at your stop. In your neighborhood the sidewalk only runs along one side of the street. As if it doesn't deserve a second sidewalk like the nicer neighborhoods have.

Your house is dark reddish brick with gray shingles and black shutters. Walking with Celeste you see things you wouldn't normally notice. The gutters overflow with dull brown leaves and bare twigs. A rolled-up dark gray, soggy, week-old newspaper lies on the walk.

"I know it's not much." You let Celeste in your house. "But it's okay for my mom and me."

"Don't be dumb." Once inside, Celeste looks around. "It's great. And look at these." She picks up one of the blue bottles that line the windowsills. "They're cool."

"Mom collects them," you tell her. "Mostly at yard sales. Hungry?"

"Starved."

She isn't kidding. In the kitchen you make her a box of macaroni and cheese, then a bowl of chunky chicken soup. When she's still hungry, you share some chocolate chip cookies.

"That was great." Celeste licks cookie crumbs off her fingertips.

"Want anything else?" You're joking, of course.

"What have you got?" She's serious.

"Uh, ice cream?"

"Sure."

You look in the freezer. "Vanilla okay?"

"With hot fudge sauce?"

"How's chocolate syrup?"

"Good enough."

You prepare two bowls, but give more of the ice cream to Celeste. She floods her bowl with chocolate syrup, then starts to wolf down the sundae in heaping spoonfuls.

"How do you stay thin?"

"My mom says I have a superfast metabolism," she answers. "I just burn up calories."

The wall phone rings. You jump up and answer. "Hello?"

"Ready?" It's Tara.

The phone cord is extra long. You stretch it out of the kitchen and into the living room where you hope Celeste won't hear. "For what?"

"We're going to the mall, remember? Christmas shopping."

"Oh, uh, I can't." You shoot a hasty glance back

through the kitchen doorway. Celeste's still spooning up vanilla ice cream with chocolate sauce.

"How come?" Tara asks.

You lower your voice to a whisper. "Know Celeste Van Warner?"

"Never heard of her," Tara deadpans.

"She's here."

"So?"

"She needs help with math."

"And you can't go to the mall," Tara says. "How sad. Poor helpless Celeste."

"Be serious. Can't we go tomorrow?"

"But what about poor helpless Celeste? Tomorrow she might need help with Spanish. Or archery. Or tying her shoes." Tara hangs up.

You start to dial Tara back but then glance into the kitchen. A spoon in an empty bowl sits on the table. Where's Celeste? You hang up the phone, go looking, and find her in your room sorting through the clothes in your closet. You catch your breath and feel humiliated. The room is a wreck—clothes all over the floor and bed. Magazines, books, CDs, and candy wrappers scattered everywhere. What a dump!

Meanwhile, from the closet Celeste pulls out a tight, low-cut black top with a gold star on the front.

"Have I seen you wear this?" she asks.

"No way." A nervous laugh bursts from your lungs. "My crazy aunt Sarah gave it to me for my birthday. She lives in Los Angeles. You know. La-la land."

Celeste holds it up to herself in the mirror. "I'd wear it."

You get the funniest feeling. Almost as if she's asking for it. "Borrow it if you like."

"Could I?" Celeste gasps.

"Sure. I mean, that's better than if it just hangs there."

"That's sooo nice," Celeste says. "Maybe you'll come over to my house and find something you'd like."

You feel your pulse jump. This is like candy to your ears. Girlfriends sharing clothes. Like they do in books and on TV shows. The A-list girls must spend hours trying on one another's things. They all have such nice clothes. You don't have much. Some jeans, a few skirts, and a bunch of tops. But no one to share them with. You're a size six and Tara is a size twelve. About the only things you can share are sweatshirts.

Celeste reaches into your closet again, this time pulling out your turquoise skating outfit with the glitter finish and flared skirt. She gives it an uncertain look.

"It's a skating outfit," you explain.

"Oh." She glances around the room, now taking in the skating posters, the little silver trophies you won when you were younger, and your first pair of skates, scuffed white, which hang from a nail on your wall.

"Been skating since I was three," you tell her. "One summer I even went to skating camp at Lake Placid."

Celeste brings a finger to her lips and chews on a fingernail. For the first time you notice that her nails are all bitten down to the nubs.

"Do you skate?" you ask.

"Not really."

Disappointment creeps under your skin. There's a new skating rink in town and you're dying to go. But Tara doesn't skate and you don't want to go alone.

Celeste looks down and, with her shoe, sorts through the magazines and clothes on your floor. She bends down and picks up a CD. "Oh, wow, I love her. Isn't she great?"

"My fav," you reply, aware that if Tara ever heard you say "fav" instead of "favorite" she'd probably drive a stake through your heart.

"Mine, too." Celeste loads the disc into your boom box. The room fills with music, and she spins on her toes and dances over to the big green ceramic piggy bank on your dresser. It's shaped like a barrel and is more than a foot tall.

She slides her arms around it and lifts slightly, almost as if she wants to dance with it. The change inside clatters.

"Careful!" you yelp, picturing the barrel slipping through her arms and smashing apart on the floor.

Leaving the piggy bank, she waltzes over to the little makeup table. She seems to need to touch everything—every piece of clothing, every CD, every eyeliner and compact. "We're going to have so much fun together," she sings to you as she twists the top off a lip gloss.

You sit on your bed and watch as if in a dream, not quite believing that this A-lister likes your clothes and taste in music and wants to be your friend. "We are?" you answer in dazed uncertainty.

Celeste stops abruptly and turns to you. The music is still playing. She crosses her arms and beneath her bangs her eyebrows dip into seriousness. The abruptness of the change catches you by surprise.

"What?" you stammer warily as if worried you just said the wrong thing and she will now vanish from your life as quickly as she appeared.

"Have I ever seen you wear makeup?" she asks.

"Huh? Uh, no."

"Why not?"

A warm shiver crawls over your skin. Dare you speak the truth? That you're dying to wear makeup but terrified someone like Krista or Stephanie will make fun of you?

"I never have time in the morning."

"Well, come on." She pats the chair at the makeup table. "Let's do it now."

"What about equivalent fractions?"

Celeste makes a face. "Oh, please." She waves the idea away. "We'll do that later."

chapter
five

"We'll go to California and find sugar daddies." Celeste kneels beside you painting fantasies in your mind and blue eye shadow on your eyelids.

"Why?"

"They'll give us money."

"Why?"

"Because they're yucky, old, wrinkly rich guys who give pretty girls like us money to hang around and make them feel good."

"We won't have to kiss them, will we?"

"Maybe on the cheek."

"Gross!"

"Oh, come on, you kiss your grandfather on his cheek, don't you?"

"I guess."

"Hold still." She adds eyeliner. "And then, when we have enough money, we'll open a boutique and get all our clothes wholesale."

"How do you know about all this stuff?"

"My mom."

"Your . . . mom?"

"Yeah. She told me she once had a sugar daddy when she was younger. But that was a long time ago. She's really different now."

"Oh."

"Hold it." She applies mascara to your lashes. No one except your mom has ever put makeup on you before. No one except your mom has ever fussed over you and made you feel so special. You imagine Celeste and you becoming the world's tightest, bestest friends. You feel like you're in a magic, Cinderella-type dream. Only here, Celeste is the prince who's discovered you.

"I'd kill for your cheekbones," she says, the mascara stick wedged between her lips, as she brushes blush on your cheeks, then gets up and stands behind you. "So what do you think?"

You stare at yourself. "I look like I'm twenty-five!" This is only a slight exaggeration.

Behind you, Celeste winks. "That's the whole idea, right?"

You can't get used to the two people in the mirror. You, looking like someone completely new, and Celeste, who is completely new. The two of you framed like a painting. A portrait of friends forever? Is this the beginning of a new life? Truth be told, that is your greatest single wish.

"I hate to say it." Celeste glances at her Swatch. "We better do our homework."

Now? Disappointment weighs down your shoulders. The fun can't end now. The music, the makeup, the hair and girl talk. It's too enjoyable to stop. You can't remember having a friend who made you feel this good. Not since Krista Rice lived across the street, back when you both were little. Back before she moved and left you behind in every way. . . .

You and Celeste sit on the floor with open notebooks. She wasn't kidding about not getting the math. You wind up doing almost all the homework yourself. Celeste plays more CDs and thumbs through magazines. Finally she looks up from the *Teen People* she's been reading. "Oh, my gosh! It's dark!"

"So?"

"I'll have to call a cab. What's the address here?"

After you tell her, she picks up her books and the low-cut black top with the gold star, and heads for the kitchen. You follow and wait while she uses the phone.

"That's lucky. There's a cab in the neighborhood." She hangs up and glances at the kitchen clock. "Won't your mom be home soon?"

"No. She works late."

"What does she do?"

You hate when people ask. "She's a waitress . . . at Carmen's. I know it doesn't sound like much, but you'd be amazed at how much she makes with tips and every-thing."

"Isn't that the place Stephanie Eisley's father owns?" Celeste asks.

You nod, wincing inside at the sound of Stephanie's name.

Celeste narrows her eyes. "So *that's* why you didn't fight back today when Stephanie cut you down. How could you? Your mother works for her father."

It's nice of her to say that, but deep down you know that even if your mom didn't work at Carmen's, you wouldn't have fought back.

You and Celeste walk through the living room. "What's with this school anyway?" she asks by the front door.

"What do you mean?"

"Some of the girls are so cruel."

"Aren't they?" You're incredibly glad that she said that. Only, aren't some of the cruelest girls also Celeste's friends? "Maybe it's just when they're with their crowd and they feel like they have to show off."

"You don't have to make excuses for them," Celeste says. "Maybe they're just bad people." A car honks out-side. It's the cab. Celeste sticks her hand in her bag and searches around. "Oh, no, where's my money?"

The cab beeps again. Celeste bites her lip and gives you a "What am I going to do?" look.

"I've got money." You race back to your room and take five dollars out of your wallet. When you return, the front door is wide open and cold air is blowing in. Celeste is down at the curb getting into the cab. You run down the front walk and hand her the money through the window.

She smiles up at you. "Well, I'm just glad I met one of the *good* people. Thanks for everything, Lauren."

"No prob, Celeste. Thank *you*."

The cab goes down the street, around the corner, and disappears into the dark. Back inside the house, your room feels empty. As if Celeste sucked the life out of it when she left. To bring back the memory of the fun you just had, you decide to put on that first CD she played. The one you both like so much. You look for a moment and can't find it. Must be buried somewhere beneath the clothes and junk.

You put on a different CD. The throbbing music helps fill the emptiness. Celeste is unlike anyone you've ever been friends with before. You can't say that you understand her completely, but you are very, very glad she came over today. You slip into the chair in front of the mirror. Once again that new, unfamiliar girl with makeup looks back at you. She is definitely prettier than you. You would like to be that girl, and you don't under-stand this sudden urge to run into the bathroom and scrub off every bit of makeup. Who are you afraid will see? There's no one here except you. Can't you be a little bit brave? Yes. You decide to be that pretty girl, just for tonight, and not wash off the makeup until you go to bed.

chapter
SIX

"You need more confidence in yourself, hon."

"I know, Mom."

"You're smart and attractive and likeable. There's no reason why you should feel this way."

"I know. It's just . . . I don't know how you get confidence. I mean, it's not like going to a gym and getting more muscles, or just waiting until I grow more hair."

"You get it by believing in yourself."

You are waiting at Tara's locker the next morning to make sure she is still your friend, when you spot Krista Rice coming down the hall with Stephanie Eisley and Judy Knight. While Krista is the ultimate DYWYWM girl, and Stephanie is the ultimate DYWYWM wanna-be, Judy is altogether different. She wears her curly black hair short and dresses plainly without a touch of makeup. The smartest person in the grade, she floats freely above the cliques, admired by, and friendly to, almost everyone.

Always invited to parties, but more likely to spend Saturday night doing homework than hanging out.

And while Krista and Stephanie must carry the latest handbags, Judy lugs a backpack heavy with books. She lives a block away from you and has a brother with muscular dystrophy who goes to a special school and needs a lot of expensive medical treatment.

As usual when the A-listers pass, you avert your eyes and pretend to be immersed in your planner. So you're caught totally off guard when Krista breaks away from the others and comes toward you.

"Lauren?"

You look up, surprised and wary. It's been years since you've heard her utter your name. "Oh, hi."

Krista's brown eyes are made darker by her makeup and tight brown shirt. She looks right into yours as she steps close and whispers, "I saw Celeste Van Warner get on the bus with you yesterday."

You're not sure how to answer. Judy and Stephanie have stopped nearby, but a polite distance away—not so close that they can hear.

"I'd be careful if I were you," Krista continues in a low voice. "There's something about her that isn't right."

"Uh, okay, thanks."

Krista's eyes have not left yours, as if she's looking for something inside you. Finally she angles back to Stephanie and Judy and those three continue down the hall. You're totally not sure what to make of this. The first time in a thousand years Krista decides to talk to you, and it turns out to be a warning about this new girl who sits at the DYWYWM table and yet wants to be your friend?

"Well, look who's here." Tara arrives with a smirk and pulls off her dull black parka with the white stitching where her mom has sewn up rips in the nylon material. Hard to believe she still wears that jacket, since it's at least two sizes too small. "That must have been a pretty short friendship."

"What are you talking about?" you ask.

"You and Celeste."

"We're still friends."

"Then how come you're waiting for me?" Tara asks.

You decide to give her a dose of her own medicine. "Oh, right, how could I be so stupid? I forgot I can only have one friend at a time. Well, see ya."

Of course, you don't leave. Tara starts to do the combination on her lock.

"Did you go to the mall?" you ask.

"No."

"How come?"

"What do you care?"

You can't believe how seriously she's taking this. "Tara, come on. You're my best friend."

She straightens up and faces you, the lines between her eyebrows deepening. "When Celeste isn't around."

"No, even when she is around. Yesterday was an exception. I just wanted to get to know her."

"Why couldn't you get to know her on another day?" Tara sniffs.

"I don't know. It wasn't like that. She needed help with math."

"And what if she needs help again today?" Tara asks. "What if she needs homework help every day?"

"She won't," you answer, although now that Tara's mentioned it, you do wish that every afternoon could be like yesterday. "Anyway I want to go to the mall with you. That is, if you still want to go."

"I'll think about it," Tara replies.

It doesn't take Tara long. By lunchtime you and she are back at your regular table in the land of the socially inferior. Celeste, wearing your black top with the gold star, is sitting at the DYWYWM table, halfway between Queen Krista in the middle and the wanna-bes at the ends.

"Isn't that your top?" Tara asks.

"She borrowed it."

"Uh-huh." Tara nods slowly.

"Uh-huh what?"

"Guess I'm just wondering. If you're such good buddies, how come you're not sitting with her?"

Funny she should ask. You've been dreaming all morning that Celeste would suggest it. "I don't know."

"Wrong answer," Tara says. "You're supposed to say, because you want to sit with me."

"Maybe someday we'll *both* sit over there."

Tara snorts. "When pigs fly."

At the DYWYWM table, Celeste looks up and catches your eye. You feel yourself start to flush with embarrassment that she caught you staring, but she gives you a little wave.

And even though you're not sitting with her, it almost feels like you are.

seven

"It really makes me mad," Celeste says about a week later at the food court in the mall. You've finally gotten up the nerve to ask her about the DYWYWM crowd. "It's so not fair. I mean, why shouldn't you sit at that table with us? Why weren't you invited to Shelby Kirk's party over the weekend?"

"Shelby had a party?" You hadn't even *heard* about it. "Who was there?"

"Oh, you know, the same old crowd." Celeste reels off the names of all the guys and girls you'd imagine would be invited. They may have been the same old crowd to her, but you are completely envious.

"I just don't understand why it has to be this way," she says.

"You mean, the way the whole grade is divided into cliques?"

She nods and reaches up to the counter to get the paper plate with her slice of pizza. It's still hard to believe you're at the mall with her. You were supposed to go home after school and do the laundry, but then Celeste came by your locker and asked if you wanted to go to the mall. So you'll do the laundry later. Your mom will understand.

"Seven fifty," says the counter man with the stained T-shirt.

Celeste searches her bag, then frowns and looks back down the corridor at the stores you've just visited.

"Forget your money again?" you ask.

"No, I can't find my wallet."

"You lost it?" This is cause for serious concern.

Celeste begins to gnaw on a fingernail. Her eyes are wide with panic. "I don't know."

"Okay, when did you last see it?" You take charge the way your mom does in an emergency.

"I don't know! I don't remember!" Completely forgetting the slices and Cokes you've just ordered, she turns toward the corridor.

"Wait!" You grab her arm. "I don't remember you taking it out since we got here. Are you sure you even brought it?"

Celeste stares at you uncertainly. She blinks twice. "I did switch bags at home today."

"So it's probably in the other bag," you conclude.

"No, I wouldn't have forgotten it."

"You sure?"

She goes limp and puts a hand on your shoulder, not

so much for support as in appreciation. "No, I'm not sure . . . Oh, Laur, I'm sorry."

"It's no problem."

She smiles weakly. "Thanks, Laur. And thanks for being so calm. That was totally freaky."

"Let's just sit down, okay?" Crisis averted, you pay for the slices and Cokes and lead her to a table. Recently she's started calling you Laur, especially when she wants to talk about something serious and personal. She's the only person who's ever called you that. As if she knows a different you than everyone else.

"I'll pay you back tomorrow," she says as you both settle into metal chairs bolted to the floor.

"Oh, stop. It's nothing. I'm just glad we know where your wallet is."

You both bite into your slices and sip your sodas. It feels good to know that in some ways she needs you as much as you need her.

After a moment, Celeste parts her bangs and looks straight at you. "How do you always have money?"

"Baby-sitting. While you were at Shelby Kirk's party on Saturday, I was watching the McGuire twins."

"Not fun." Celeste shakes her head.

"It's not so bad. I'm in demand. So if a kid gives me a hard time I just don't baby-sit him anymore. There's always someone else who wants me."

"How much do you get?"

You tell her, and she wrinkles her brow. "That's *all?*"

Her comment stings. You thought it was pretty good for a kid your age. "Don't forget. Three or four times a week adds up."

Celeste leans toward you, dropping her voice. "How much do you have?"

You're caught off guard by this awfully personal question. Even Tara has never asked. Then you think about all the other private things you and Celeste have shared over the past week. Things that feel way more personal than money.

Across the table, Celeste shakes her head. "I shouldn't have asked. It's none of my business."

"I don't care," you tell her. "If you want to know the truth, I have more money than I know what to do with. You know that big piggy jar? It must have four hundred dollars in it."

"No way," Celeste says. "I picked it up. It didn't weigh that much."

You grin proudly. "That's because it's not in change. It's mostly fives, tens, and twenties."

eight

"Why don't you run for student government?" Mom asks.

"Why would I do that?"

"You're smart and capable. I think you'd be good at it."

"It's just a popularity contest, Mom."

"There has to be more to it than that, hon. It's about responsibility."

"Right. You get to pick themes for the spirit days and organize the holiday party and the spring dance. You'll see. I'll bet anything no one even dares to run against Krista for president."

"Don't you just love it?" Celeste gazes at a choker made of four strands of dark silverish beads in the display counter at Silverstone's Accessories. You're at the mall again. For you it's fun. But for Celeste it seems to be more than that. It's almost as if she *has* to go.

"I could never wear that," you say.

"Of course you could."

"No way."

"Why not?"

"Because . . ."

"Because you're afraid of what someone might say?" You feel your face turn red with shame.

Celeste clamps her hands on her hips. "You can't be like that, Laur. You're pretty and smart and just as good as anyone else." She waves at a saleslady who's standing down at the other end of the counter. "Excuse me."

You're gripped by sudden panic. *"What are you doing?"*

"I'm buying it for you."

The saleslady is coming. "Can I help you?"

"You can't!" You whisper under your breath.

"Try and stop me." Celeste turns to the saleslady. "I'd like to see this choker."

"No!" you blurt.

The saleslady scowls.

"Don't listen to her," Celeste says.

"No! Don't listen to *her!*" You grab Celeste by the arm and start to drag her away from the counter. "She doesn't know what she's talking about. She must be on drugs."

"I am not!" Celeste cries, and pulls back. "I just want to do something for a friend."

"Well, not that!" You pull harder.

The saleslady crosses her arms and gives you both an impatient, annoyed look. You're just a couple of kids fooling around and wasting her time. She turns to help someone else.

Outside Silverstone's, you and Celeste are red-faced and giggling.

"Did you see the look she gave us?" You chortle.

"She wouldn't have, if you'd let me buy you that stupid choker," Celeste answers.

"You're not buying me anything. If I want something, I can buy it myself."

"The only thing you'd buy is a nun's habit," she teases, slipping her arm through yours. Arm in arm you stroll down the corridor. "Come on, prude, when are you going to loosen up?"

"Probably when I run away from this dumb town," you mutter.

"No!" Celeste stops and puts her hands on your shoulders and stares sternly into your eyes. "Never say that! That's just what they *want* you to do. You're going to stay and fight, Laur. Promise?"

You nod, surprised, but delighted that she feels so strongly. "Promise."

Next stop is Baskin-Robbins for ice cream. Celeste tries to treat you, but they don't accept credit cards.

"Know what we should do?" she asks between licks of her pink bubble-gum ice-cream cone. "Run for student government."

"*You* could."

"You, too," she goes.

"Not a chance."

"Uh-oh, is this like the choker?"

You stare down at your French vanilla cone and feel your face start to heat up.

"You have to believe in yourself, Laur."

That's weird. It's the same thing your mom said. "I do. I believe that if I ran . . . I wouldn't get five votes."

"What if we run together?" Celeste asks. "Walsh and Van Warner for president and vice president."

"Against Krista and Judy? Are you out of your mind?"

Celeste slides a fingernail between her lips. "What about secretary and treasurer?"

Before you can answer, she changes her mind. "No, forget about secretary. All you do is take notes at the meetings. And then you're supposed to type them up and read them back before the next meeting."

"Too much work?"

"*Way* too much work." Celeste licks her bright pink ice-cream cone. "Hey, why don't we *both* run for treasurer?"

"Against each other?"

"No, silly, like co-treasurers. You're good at math and I'm good at—"

You fill in the blank: "Being liked."

chapter
nine

"Mom?"

"Yes, hon?"

"There's, uh, something I need to tell you."

"Don't be shy."

"I've decided to run for class treasurer."

"That's wonderful! Why do you look so worried? Are you afraid you'll lose?"

"Well, it's not that. I mean, I guess I should be worried about that, too. But it's something else."

"I'm listening."

"I'm running against Stephanie."

"Mr. Eisley's daughter?"

"Yeah, Mom. I'm sorry."

"You don't have to be sorry, hon. I'm sure Mr. Eisley will understand. It's a free country. Anyone who wants to can run for office."

"Sure, but . . ."

"It's not your concern. You do whatever you want."

"Thanks, Mom."

* * *

You're standing on a chair in the hall, taping one of the posters you've made to the wall above your locker.

"Good for you," someone says.

You look down at a head of short, curly light brown hair. It's Rob Carlucci, a thin boy who wears glasses, preppy khakis, and light blue shirts with collars.

"You think?"

"Sure, why not?"

"I've never done anything like this."

"Then it's about time." Rob lives across the street from you in the house where Krista once lived. Rob always has a smile and something nice to say. He's one of the few popular boys who isn't a big jock or a big jerk. He's just friendly to everyone and seems very sure of himself.

"You don't think Stephanie will be mad?"

"No madder than I am at Shelby Kirk since she decided to run for secretary."

"How mad's that?"

Rob shoves his hands into his pockets. "Zero mad. Whoever wins, wins. There's no hard feelings. So what made you decide to do it?"

"It was Celeste's idea, really. She'll shake hands and I'll crunch numbers."

"Sounds like a plan." Rob grins. "I hope you win, Lauren. I really do."

There's something in his voice you've never heard before. You're not sure what it means, but it makes your ears feel warm.

"Thanks, Rob."

He lingers in the hall a moment more, gazing up at you. "Well, guess I better go. Let me know if I can help, okay?"

"Okay."

He heads off down the hall and you watch, wondering what that was about. But then the tape comes off on the upper corner of the poster and you have to restick it before the whole thing falls. With your back to the hall, you are uncomfortably aware that kids are stopping to look.

"Walsh and Van Warner for co-treasurers?" You know the voice. It's Tara.

"Hi." You twist around, feeling guilty. It's been days since you two spoke. Instead of going to the cafeteria at lunch, you've been making posters in the art room.

"What is this?" Tara asks.

"It's what I've been doing at lunch instead of eating in the cafeteria," you explain.

"Oh. I thought you didn't want to be seen with me anymore." The sharp, perceptive words jab into you. "Why didn't you just tell me?"

"Celeste wanted it to be a surprise." You step down from the chair.

"Well, you can definitely forget about being invited to Stephanie's next pizza party." This is a joke, since you've never been invited anyway.

"Guess that's a price I'll have to pay."

"Seriously, Lauren. You're sure you want to do it?"

"Why not?"

"Maybe because it's totally obvious you're riding on Celeste's coattails."

That hurts. You know Tara is just calling it the way she sees it. But still, she's supposed to be your friend. You lower your voice. "Can I tell you a secret?"

"Why not?"

"I'm only doing it because Celeste needs someone who's good at math."

"Uh-huh." Tara gives you an exaggerated, disbelieving nod.

"It's true!" you insist.

"You are too much, Lauren."

She's angry and hurt. She's always been a good friend. Until recently, the only one you had. "What are you doing after school today?" you ask.

"Uh, let me guess. Helping you make more posters?"

"If you want."

"What about your co-treasurer?"

"She has a doctor's appointment."

Tara chuckles. "Why am I not surprised?"

By week's end you've put up three times as many posters as Stephanie. So many that one teacher teases that you could have a career in wallpapering. Back in the cafeteria for the first time in a week, you gaze at the DYWYWM table. Celeste is deep in conversation with Judy Knight. The only person who meets your gaze is Krista.

"Lauren!" Tara grunts irritably.

"Sorry." You look down at today's lunch. Mom packed a tuna fish sandwich. The oil has seeped out and stained the brown paper bag, leaving your backpack and books smelling fishy.

"I thought for sure you'd be sitting over there by now," Tara says.

"Not without you."

"Gee, I didn't know you cared."

Tara's nonstop sarcasm grates, but still, she's your best friend. Carefully using the tips of your fingers, you unwrap the tuna sandwich. The fishy scent grows stronger. The DYWYWM girls don't smell of fish. Tomorrow, you decide, you will buy lunch.

"Lauren?" Tara says.

"Hmmm?"

"This is just a suggestion, but you might want to tell Celeste to be a little less obvious about copying homework out of your notebook in the library."

You feel your face start to glow.

"If she gets caught, you'll get in trouble, too," Tara says. "Why do you let her?"

"I didn't actually know."

"You didn't know she had your notebook?"

"Well, yes, she asked to borrow it. I just . . . didn't ask why."

Tara gives you a truly scathing look. You shrug meekly. It's hard to explain this to her. "It's just . . . we're getting friendly, you know?"

"If you're getting so friendly, how come she never sits with us?"

You look up from your smelly sandwich and across the table at Tara. She's wearing a white sweatshirt with a light brown stain on the front. Not a new stain that she's just gotten that day, but an old washed-a-hundred-times stain. How can you tell her that you know *exactly* why Celeste doesn't sit at your table? For the same reason you wouldn't sit there either, if you had the choice.

"Can I give you some advice?" Tara asks.

"Okay."

"Be careful with her. There's something about her I don't trust."

That's odd, because it's the same thing Krista said. But you don't mention that because you know they're both wrong. The truth is, neither of them really knows Celeste. Not the way you do.

eleven

"How's the campaign going?" Mom asks.

"Good. I have to tell you the funniest thing. I got a 98 on a math quiz, and Mr. Youngstrom told the whole class that if they vote for me they won't have to worry about the class bank account."

"That's great, hon."

"And Stephanie was sitting right there!"

"Oops!" Mom smiles.

Something has changed. You can feel it. Yesterday Judy Knight, who's running for vice-president, stopped you in the hall and said she liked your posters. A-list girls like Shelby Kirk, who never even looked in your direction before, now smile at you. Even the hot boys, like Reed Palmer, seem to notice you.

You hardly sleep the night before the election. At school you see Celeste in the girls' locker room before gym.

"Did you write up the science lab?" she asks in a low voice.

"Here. I made you a copy." You pull the lab write-up from your science folder and hand it to her. You're not in the same science class, but you both have the same teacher, Ms. Dillsen, and she gives the same homework. "I changed the numbers a little, but the results are still the same, okay?"

"Thanks, Laur, you're a real friend. So, think we have a chance today?"

"Who knows?"

"Two girls told me this morning they're going to vote for us because they don't want Stephanie to win."

"Great! The 'We-Hate-Stephanie' vote!"

You both giggle and start to change for gym. Secretly you estimate that if half the popular kids vote for Celeste and a lot of the social outcasts vote for you, you have a shot at winning.

The vote is held at lunchtime. They make everyone line up in the hall outside the cafeteria and cast ballots before they can go in. Otherwise, the only kids who'd vote would be the candidates and their friends.

Waiting in line with Tara, you look around for Celeste. You don't see her or the other A-list girls, but once again the kids you do see act differently. Those who once looked away now smile or nod.

Rob Carlucci strolls up, hands in the pockets of his khaki slacks, a relaxed expression on his face. "Hey, Tara. Hey, Lauren. Who're you guys gonna vote for?"

"Don't know," Tara answers. "Just can't make up my mind."

"How can you be so calm?" you ask him. "Aren't you just a little nervous?"

"That Shelby Kirk might beat me for secretary and then she'll get stuck taking all the notes and typing them up?" Rob chuckles. "Do me a favor, vote for her, okay?"

He's kidding, of course. But you're struck by how relaxed he is. He could lose and it really wouldn't bother him.

"So, Lauren," he says. "If elected, just what do you plan to do for our grade?"

"I intend . . ." you begin in a whisper, "to throw the biggest party this school has ever seen!"

"Sounds good to me." Tara lifts her hand as if to share a hi-five, but then sees something and stops abruptly. You turn and see Stephanie Eisley coming down the line toward you, her long streaked blond hair parted in the middle and flapping slightly like a pair of wings.

Expecting a nasty cut down, you feel yourself start to freeze.

Stephanie stops. "Hi, Rob, Lauren, Tara."

"Uh-oh!" Rob grins. "Fight fair, girls. No eye gouging or hair pulling."

"Lauren." Stephanie focuses on you. "I just hope that no matter which of us wins, there'll be no hard feelings, okay?"

You nod mutely, still bracing for the nastiness that's sure to follow. But it doesn't come.

"You mean, no fight?" Rob pretends to be disappointed.

"Sorry, Rob." Stephanie turns around and heads toward the back of the line.

"Guess I better get on line, too," Rob says. "Otherwise I'll never get to eat. See ya later."

He follows Stephanie. You're still in shock. Is it possible that Stephanie Eisley, the girl who only a few weeks ago had no problem cutting you down to tears in front of everyone, is now making sure you two won't be enemies?

"Now I've seen everything," Tara mutters.

"Running for class government sure changes things," you observe.

"Not quite," Tara whispers. "Running with Celeste Van Warner is what changes things."

twelve

You and Tara vote, then go into the cafeteria and sit at your usual spot among the undesirables. But when you look over at the DYWYWM table, Celeste flashes a hopeful thumbs-up sign. Even Krista smiles.

"Don't let me stop you," Tara grumbles as she peels the wrapper off the first beef jerky of the day.

She's right. The A-list girls have made it more obvious than ever that it will be okay if you sit with them. All you have to do is get up and go.

"Would you go, too?" you ask Tara.

"Give me a break," she replies. "Don't make this a big deal, Lauren, just go."

You are dying to go but also frightened. What if Shelby Kirk and Stephanie decide to get mean? What if all the other kids in the cafeteria see? And what about Tara? Can you really get up and leave her there alone? Inside you are torn by what you know you want, what still scares you, and what you know is right. It's the golden rule. You would hate it if Tara were to leave you sitting by yourself. Is that what it takes to be a DYWYWM girl? The ability to think only of yourself? But look at Celeste. She thinks of you.

"Attention, students, for an announcement from Principal Hansen." Toward period's end, the cafeteria loudspeaker crackles, then your principal comes on. "I have the results of the student government election. Krista Rice, president. Judy Knight, vice president. Rob Carlucci, secretary. And for treasurer . . . Lauren Walsh and Celeste Van Warner."

The bell rings. The announcement always comes just before the end of the period so that the losers can disappear into the crowd of kids moving to their next class. All around the cafeteria kids rise and strap on their backpacks.

"Well, congratulations, Lauren." Tara starts to get up. "Aren't you coming?"

"In a moment." You're still sitting.

Tara follows your eyes to the DYWYWM table. "Right. See you later." She heads out.

A moment later you do get up, but you time it so that you join Celeste and the others near the exit as they leave the cafeteria.

"Congratulations," Celeste says.

"Congratulations to *you*, co-treasurer," you reply.

"Congratulations, Lauren," adds Krista. "We're going to meet in the band room after school today. See you then?"

"Definitely." *You're in! You've done it!*

After school, you're the first to arrive in the band room. Since this meeting isn't a class one has to be on time for, the A-listers will arrive "fashionably late." You even know precisely where they are—in the girls' room fixing their hair and makeup.

Celeste is the next to arrive. With broad smiles you congratulate each other again.

"Can you believe how lucky we are?" she asks. "We only beat Stephanie by five votes."

"Really?" That's a lot closer than you expected.

"Guess she still has a lot of friends," Celeste says. "But, hey, we won, and that's all that counts, right?"

"Right!"

Krista comes in with Judy and Rob. You all move chairs into a circle. Rob opens his laptop computer. You all wait for Krista to speak, but Krista also waits.

"Ready," Rob says.

"I just thought it would be a good idea if we got down to business right away," Krista says, very businesslike. Her words are echoed by the rapid clicking of Rob's fingers on his laptop. "The last Friday of every month is a spirit day. We already know that everybody loves pajama day, hippie day, school color day, and dress-up day. But that still leaves four months. Any other suggestions?"

"Underwear day?" Rob suggests.

"You'd just love that," Krista says with a smirk.

"What about bathing-suit day?" Celeste suggests.

Krista and Judy exchange approving looks. You wish you could have thought of that.

"Let's do it in February," Rob says.

"The last Friday in May." Krista jots it down on her Palm Pilot. She, Judy, Celeste, and Rob bat around a few more possibilities. You remain quiet. Not that you're being shy. If you had a good idea you'd suggest it. But everything you think of seems dumb.

The rest of the spirit days are finally decided and Krista moves on to the holiday party.

"Any suggestions?" she asks.

"I know one thing," Judy says. "It's not going to be another swimming party."

"Why not?" Celeste asks.

"You weren't here last year, so you don't know what a disaster it was," Krista says. She looks around and her gaze settles on you. Her brow furrows slightly. "Were you there, Lauren?"

You shake your head.

"Smart," Krista says, although you both know that the reason you weren't there had nothing to do with being smart. Tara, being heavy, refuses to be seen in a bathing suit. And without your closest friend, you couldn't see yourself going to the party either.

"Not only was it freezing," Krista explains to Celeste, "but the boys decided it would be fun to throw the girls in, whether they wanted to go in or not."

"A lot of wet hair?" Celeste guesses.

Judy pretends to shiver at the memory. "What a nightmare."

"So," Krista says, twirling her brown hair on her finger thoughtfully, "any *other* ideas?"

"That don't involve dancing," Rob adds.

You have an idea. "How about an ice-skating party?"

Krista shows a raised eyebrow's worth of interest.

Inspired, you continue. "They just opened that new rink in town. So it should be nice."

"Sounds like fun," says Judy.

"*If* you like to skate," Rob points out.

"They also have a video arcade," you quickly add.

"Cool." Rob instantly brightens.

Judy turns to Krista. "Doesn't Peter play hockey? Maybe you could get him to come."

Krista's face goes blank. "You're joking, right?" she replies in a chilly monotone.

Nothing more is said about the mysterious Peter.

"Won't it be expensive?" Celeste asks in her new role as co-treasurer.

"Do you know what it costs, Lauren?" Krista asks.

"No," you answer. "But since the rink's brand new I

bet the owners would give us a good deal, because once the kids go there they'll want to come back."

"Hey, *someone's* thinking," Rob says, and you feel yourself flush with pride at the compliment.

"Does anyone know what's in the class fund?" Krista asks.

Judy flips through a notebook. "A little over five hundred dollars."

"Good." Krista turns to Celeste and you. "As our new co-treasurers, your first job will be to find out how much it will cost to rent the skating rink. Try to get them to give you a good price."

thirteen

"Congratulations on winning, hon."

"Wait, Mom, it gets better. They needed an idea for the class party. I suggested skating and they liked it."

"That's wonderful. And all that time you thought they didn't like you."

"Well, I'm just a co-treasurer."

"You're the one who said it was a popularity contest. Have they ever seen you skate?"

"I don't think so."

"I think they're going to be very impressed."

"Laur." In the middle of a math test, Celeste's whisper sends a startled shiver down your spine. As much as you enjoy the attention she gives you, this is one time when you wish she'd leave you alone. When she first came to the class in October, Celeste sat at a desk two rows over. But recently she moved to the desk next to yours.

You glance nervously at Mr. Youngstrom, sitting at his desk, his head bent as he marks tests from another class. You turn slightly and give Celeste a quick look. Just as you feared, she motions you to move your test to the right side of your desk, where she can see it.

You feel your stomach tighten. Your heart starts to pound uncomfortably. You've never cheated on a test, nor helped anyone else cheat. Maybe you've helped Celeste with her homework. Maybe you've even done her homework for her. But this is different. If you get caught, you'll be in megatrouble.

Mr. Youngstrom's head stays bowed as he concentrates on marking.

"*Laur?*" Celeste whispers again. You're not just worried about getting caught. You know this is really wrong. You should say no. But how do you say no to someone you owe so much to?

With a sour, uneasy feeling in your stomach, you slide your test to the side of your desk. Not daring to look at Celeste, you can't help hearing the feverish scratching of her pencil as she copies your answers.

And that's when the loudspeaker over the door crackles: "Lauren Walsh and Celeste Van Warner, please come to Principal Hansen's office at the end of the period."

For a moment, you can't breathe. Your heart may have been banging before, but now it booms in your chest, each beat like the thunderous blast of a cannon. It feels like it will burst and your life will end right there in math class. You grab your test and slide it back to the center of your desk, just as Mr. Youngstrom raises his head and nods at you and Celeste.

The rest of the class continues taking the test. Mr. Youngstrom goes back to marking. You steal another glance at Celeste. She widens her eyes for a second, then shakes her head as if to say, "That was freaky, but it's okay, nothing happened."

She's right. The announcement was a coincidence. Gradually your heart slows down and stops banging.

Math ends. You hand in your test and walk with a quickened step out into the hall. It's not that you're so eager to see Principal Hansen. It's just that you *have* to get out of Mr. Youngstrom's room and away from the crime you've just committed. Celeste comes out with a guilty grin on her lips. You start to feel a little better. You got away with it, and Celeste is still your friend.

"Can you believe that?" you gasp. "For a second I was sure we'd been caught!"

Celeste presses a finger to her lips. "Shush!" She doesn't seem nearly as rattled as you.

"So what do you think Principal Hansen wants?" you ask as you both start down the hall toward the office. "I mean, we can't really be in trouble, right?" Even now you can't quite shake the guilt.

Celeste shrugs. "We'll see."

"Every year I give this speech to the new treasurer," Principal Hansen begins a few minutes later, in her office. She is a tall, stern-looking woman with black hair that curls under her chin, framing her face in an oval shape. Her black eyebrows are tweezed into thin crescents over each eye. Everything about her is serious, including her serious gray suit. But you've always suspected that behind that stern outside is a nicer, softer inside that she tries to keep hidden. Once, when you saw her catch some boys plugging up a water fountain with gum, it almost looked like she was going to laugh, but she got control of herself and acted somber and principal-like instead.

The principal slides a large index-size card across the desk toward you and Celeste. "You are taking over the most responsible job in student government. You'll be in charge of the money. I hope you'll take this job seriously."

You and Celeste lean forward and look at the card. On the top the words *FIRST NATIONAL BANK* are printed in large fancy letters. Then come two paragraphs of single-spaced small print.

"This is a signature card," Principal Hansen explains. "Each year the new treasurer signs it and I send it to the bank. Before you can take out any money, the teller will compare the signatures on the withdrawal slip to the signatures on this card to make sure you're really who you say you are. Since you're co-treasurers, you'll *both* have to sign each time you withdraw money. If there's ever a problem, you can always talk to my husband. He's an officer of the bank. Any questions?"

You and Celeste shake your heads. Principal Hansen hands you a pen. You both sign the signature card. You are now official.

chapter
fourteen

"Isn't it weird that Principal Hansen's husband is a police-man?" you ask Celeste. School is over and you're back at the mall. You've never known anyone who loved to shop as much as Celeste. Every time you two go, she finds something to fall in love with, but never buys anything. At least, not when she's with you. The only thing she's ever come close to buying was that choker.

Celeste gives you a puzzled look. "No, he isn't."

"She said he's an officer at the bank."

"That just means he works there. The officers are the ones who sit at the desks." She studies you for a moment. "Have you ever been inside a bank, Laur?"

You have to think about this. "Depends on what you mean."

Celeste parts her bangs and gives you a close look.

"I mean," you go on, "I've been inside the front door. Like where the ATMs are. But not *really* inside."

"Okay, here's how it works," Celeste explains. "The tellers are the ones who sit behind the plastic windows.

When you want to put money in the bank, you give it to them. And when you want to take it out, they give it back to you. The officers usually sit at desks. They're in charge of more important things, like making loans and opening accounts, and they're the only ones who can get into the vault."

"Where they keep the money?"

"Right—Ohmygod!" She stops and stares into a display window outside a boutique called Sherman's. A mannequin there is wearing a long brown coat and the cutest maroon knit cap. "Don't you just love it?" She grabs your hand and pulls you inside.

"Why don't you get it?" you ask a few moments later while she tries it on in front of a mirror.

"I really should." But then she stops, and for a long moment she is no longer looking at herself in the cap, but at something else . . . something in the mirror that you can't see. She takes the cap off. "No."

"I don't get it," you go. "How come you never buy anything for yourself?"

"I'm always afraid I'll get home and hate it," she answers.

"So? You'll just return it. Any anyway, why would you hate this? It looks great on you."

"You think?" She tries it on again, studying herself in the mirror for a long time. You truly do not understand what the problem is.

"Laur?"

"Yes?" you answer.

"Do people ever talk about me?"

"Like how?"

"You know what I mean. Like, what do they say?"

"Well, nothing *bad.*" Except Tara, you think to yourself. But that's just jealousy. And what Krista said a few weeks ago—that there was something about Celeste that wasn't right.

"You sure?" Celeste asks.

"Uh-huh. I mean, why would they?"

"Who knows? I guess because I'm new, and people always talk about the new girl."

"Well, I'll let you know if I hear anything," you joke.

Once again Celeste takes off the cap.

"You're not going to get it?" you ask, disappointed.

"I'll think about it," she replies. The mood has changed and grown heavier. The lighthearted gleefulness is gone. You leave Sherman's together.

"What's bothering you, Celeste?"

She gives you a reluctant look and then sighs. "It's that crowd. Krista and Stephanie and the rest of them. I know some of the girls are jealous of me. I mean, especially the ones who aren't really popular. Like, they've been around here forever and they're still not really in that crowd. They'll probably never be in it. But I'm here for less than two months and I am. Know what I mean?"

Do you ever.

"There are bound to be people who are jealous of you," you answer. "But no one says anything mean. Really, Celeste." Did you ever think you'd find yourself consoling someone else for being popular?

Out in the corridor Celeste stops and turns to you with the most serious expression. "You'll tell me if anyone does say anything?"

"Uh, sure."

"Promise?" She's *really* serious.

"Promise."

fifteen

"Mom, I just called the skating rink and made an appointment to talk to the owner about the party."

"Did he sound interested?"

"Totally. I said we'd have two hundred kids."

"That's great, hon. Talking to the owner is a very grown-up thing to do."

"I know, but I'm a little scared, Mom. I've never discussed 'business' before."

"You'll do fine, hon."

On the day of the appointment, you get to school early and wait at Celeste's locker. You spot her coming down the hall with Krista and Reed Palmer. Reed is a "hottie," tall and slim with black hair and dark eyes and a dreamy smile that makes girls melt and giggle. He, Krista, and Celeste are talking and laughing.

So much for Krista's warning that there was something "not right" about Celeste. It's clear that she was just jealous and wanted Celeste for herself.

Then you notice that Celeste is wearing the maroon knit cap from Sherman's.

"So you bought it," you say.

"Bought what?" Celeste stops. Her eyes follow yours and she reaches up and touches the cap. "Oh, right, I . . . I went back and got it. So, what's up?"

"We have to go to the skating rink after school and talk to the owner about the party."

"A skating party?" Reed raises a thick dark eyebrow. "Sounds cool."

Krista's eyes dart toward Celeste. She takes Reed by the arm. "We better go."

She leads him away. Meanwhile, Celeste slides a finger between her lips and starts to gnaw. "You're going to kill me, Laur. I totally forgot that I have a doctor's appointment after school today. Think you could go without me?"

That's the last thing you want to do. "Uh, sure. Don't worry about it."

Celeste puts her hand on your shoulder. "You're great, Laur."

The bell rings and you head for homeroom in a terrible mood. It's not Celeste's fault. Everyone forgets things.

At lunch you ask Tara if she'll go with you to the skating rink.

"What happened to your co-treasurer?" she asks,

glancing over at the DYWYWM table where Celeste and the others are chatting away.

"Doctor's appointment."

Tara chews thoughtfully on a beef jerky. "I heard Stephanie's thinking of inviting you to her next pizza party."

"Liar. Celeste and I beat her for treasurer. Stephanie must hate me. She's the *last* person who'd invite me to anything."

"I don't think that's the way she looks at it," Tara replies. "If you beat her in the election it means she almost *has* to invite you to the party."

"Why?" you ask, honestly puzzled.

"Because if you beat her, then you must be somebody," Tara explains, like it's incredibly obvious. "I mean, do you think Stephanie Eisley could bear the thought of being beaten by a nobody?"

In the weird, twisted logic of popularity, this apparently makes sense. You pretend to shrug the news off. Partly because you're not sure you believe it. And partly because, if it's true, you don't want Tara to see how excited you are.

After school it's one of those strange, unseasonably warm, sunny winter days. Your brain has a hard time matching the bare tree branches and dull brown grass with the balmy air and people wearing their sleeves rolled up. As you and Tara walk toward the new skating rink with your jackets tucked into your backpacks, you explain what you pray will happen. "I'm really hoping the owner will give us a discount on the party in exchange for bringing so many kids."

"Sounds good to me," Tara responds.

"Think you could do it?"

"Do what?"

"Talk to him."

Tara stops walking. "Wait a minute. I don't skate. I wouldn't go to this stupid party if you paid me."

"I know, Tar, but it would be a really big help. I mean, you *always* know what to say."

"Oh, okay." Tara gives in easily. She doesn't mind talking to grown-ups. And maybe she likes being needed.

The new skating rink is in a building with blue walls and a silver roof made out of wavy metal like Ruffles potato chips. Inside, the skating rink office is cold and bare. The owner, Mr. Johnson, sits behind a plain brown desk and wears a heavy white-and-brown Norwegian sweater and a gray wool cap. He has a thick gray beard and a round, friendly face. A small space heater sits on the floor, aimed at his chair. The coils inside it glow bright reddish orange, but the room is still chilly enough to make you and Tara put your jackets on before you sit down in the wooden chairs. Today you didn't need your jackets outside, but you sure do in here.

When "talking business," Tara puts on an amazing performance. She seems to know all the right things to say: "It's not just when the kids come to the party. It's all the times they'll come back and bring their friends. A party like this will jump-start word of mouth. It'll really help increase your business."

"I'm very impressed with your argument," Mr. Johnson replies with a bemused smile as if he is also charmed by this young lady who uses words like *jump-start* and phrases like *word of mouth*. "And I would be delighted to have your party here. My only problem is that I can't close the skating rink for a whole evening just for your party. Even if it means a lot of business, I can't afford to turn away other people who might want to use the rink."

A wave of disappointment crashes down on you. First, because the skating party was your idea and now no one will know that you thought of it. And second, because you wanted everyone to see you skate. Of course you know both reasons sound selfish, but you sincerely believe that everyone else would have enjoyed the skating party, too. Only now it's not going to happen.

Mr. Johnson pulls open the top drawer of his desk and takes out two thin red-and-white coupon books. "To show you how much I appreciate you wanting to have your party here, why don't you take some discount passes for you and your families."

He slides the coupon books across the desk. You give Tara a miserable look. It's not the coupon books you want. It's the party. Now, as your second official act as school co-treasurer, you'll have to go back to Krista and tell her you've failed. You take one of the coupon books and start to get up.

"Suppose we only rent *half* the rink?" Tara suddenly asks. "You can put some plastic cones right through the middle. Then we can have our party on one side and the public can still use the other. Not only that, but when they see the party, they'll think of having parties here, too."

Mr. Johnson blinks. "Why . . . that is a fantastic idea! And since you'll only be renting half the rink, you can have it for a better price."

With Tara negotiating, Mr. Johnson agrees on three hundred dollars, including skate rentals and some tokens for the arcade games and coupons for the snack bar.

A few minutes later, outside the rink, you hug Tara. "You are a genius! What would I do without you?"

"Think we could stop at the mall?" she asks.

Oh, no . . . Of all the things she could have suggested, why that? You've been there *way* too many times lately and you have things to do at home. But how can you say no? It's simple: You can't.

Luckily the bus from the skating rink to the mall takes only a few minutes and in almost no time you're helping Tara with her Christmas shopping. It's so weird. Before you got friendly with Celeste, you probably came here once a month. Now you're here so often you're surprised the salespeople don't wave and call out your name as you pass.

Tara is looking in the window of the Toy Express for gifts for her cousins when you hear familiar voices. In the mirror behind a tall Lego display, you spot a group on the other side of the broad corridor—Krista, Celeste, Reed Palmer, and his best friend Jason Buckley.

"I thought she had a doctor's appointment," Tara says when she sees who you're staring at in the mirror.

"Tara, turn around," you whisper almost frantically.

"You don't want them to see us?"

"*Please,* Tara."

She lets out a big sigh and turns. You both stand there, watching in the mirror until the others are far down the corridor.

"I want to go home," you announce.

"We just got here," Tara protests.

"You can stay if you like."

"Lauren . . ."

You're already walking away.

Behind you Tara calls, "What's *wrong* with you?"

You feel like crying. But maybe you shouldn't be so upset. Maybe Celeste did have a doctor's appointment and came to the mall after it was over. Or maybe the appointment was canceled. But inside you know that's not what happened. It all seems so clear now. Why Krista had acted so awkwardly and had pulled Reed away that morning in the hallway.

"You're crying," Tara says on the bus home.

"Thanks, I hadn't noticed."

"Hey, don't be mad at me."

"Sorry."

You don't say another word for the rest of the ride home. Tara gets off first.

"See you tomorrow?" she asks.

"Sure." If you don't kill yourself first.

chapter
sixteen

You're too old to be called a latchkey kid, but not too old to feel like one. You wish you could call Mom at Carmen's, but it's not like she has a job at a desk and can chat on the phone. It's dinnertime and you know she's hustling around taking orders and carrying heavy trays.

Should you call Celeste and ask her why she lied? No, that would only make her angry with you. Instead, you lose yourself in television and homework. Then the phone rings. Heave yourself up. It's either Mom calling to check up or Tara. Or possibly a kid from school who isn't sure what the homework is.

"Laur?" It's Celeste and instantly you are thrown into a thick soup of confusion and speechlessness.

"Hello? Laur?"

"Uh, I'm here."

"Was that you at the mall today?"

"I guess."

"I thought so! Krista said she didn't think so, but I did."

"What happened to your doctor's appointment?"

"Would you believe I had the wrong date written down? So you know me. A free afternoon and—"

"You just had to go to the mall." You end the sentence for her and suddenly feel a rush of relief. She didn't lie!

"And I ran into Krista and those guys. So, did you find anything good?"

"No, I was just tagging along with Tara. What about you?"

"You know. Always looking, never buying."

"Except the cap."

"Right. So what happened with the skating rink?"

"Celeste, you won't believe it. The owner really loved the idea of the party, but he said he couldn't close the rink to the public."

"Oh, no! What did you do?"

"Well, I didn't know what to do . . ." you begin. "And then I . . . had . . . this idea. Like, what if we only rented *half* the rink? So we could have the party and the public could still use the other half."

"And?"

"Well, I also figured that renting half the rink wouldn't be as expensive as renting the whole rink."

"And?"

"He agreed. And he's going to throw in the skate rentals and some other stuff, too."

"Laur, that's great! You're a genius!"

chapter
seventeen

"*What's wrong, hon?*"

"*Nothing.*"

"*How did it go at the ice-skating rink?*"

"*Good. We can use it for the party.*"

"*That's wonderful. You must be very proud of yourself.*"

"*Whatever.*"

Another meeting in the band room after school. You all sit in a circle with notebooks on your laps. Except Rob, who has his laptop computer, and Krista with her Palm Pilot.

"Celeste and Lauren," Krista begins, "can you give us an update on the skating party?"

"We've got the rink," Celeste reports, and then goes on to tell them how you made this great deal with the owner. "I hate to say it, but I had nothing to do with it. Lauren handled the whole thing herself."

"Way to go, Lauren," cheers Judy Knight.

Krista also nods appreciatively.

"Good thinking, Lauren," Rob chimes in. "Renting half the rink was a stroke of genius."

You force a weak smile onto your lips. Both Celeste and Rob have now called you a genius. And it's all based on a lie. You can't believe you didn't just tell them the truth. Well, that itself is a lie. You can believe it. But really, it's not the worst lie, is it? It's not like Tara would have ever gotten the credit. Or done anything with it. This way you'll get the credit. And once you're really comfortable with this crowd, you'll bring Tara in.

"Judy, you're good at decorations," Krista says. "Can I put you in charge of them for the skating party?"

"Sure." Judy agrees.

"Could I do the decorations, too?" Celeste suddenly asks.

"Think you'll need help?" Krista asks Judy.

"All the help I can get," Judy answers.

"Can I help, too?" you ask.

"No way, Lauren," Krista says. "We all saw the posters you made for treasurer. We'll need you to do a whole bunch for the party."

You feel both disappointed and flattered. It's nice that Krista thinks you're so good at making posters. But the meeting ends and Krista, Celeste, and Judy immediately start talking about the decorations. Once again you feel left out. Not knowing what else to do, you pick up your backpack and go out into the hall.

"Lauren?" Rob comes out behind you, his black computer bag slung over his shoulder. "That really was good thinking. I *never* would have thought of dividing the rink in half."

"Oh, uh, thanks." What a bittersweet feeling—accepting a compliment you don't deserve.

Together you walk down the hall. Rob checks his watch. "It's gonna be awhile till the late bus leaves. I know it's kind of far, but you feel like walking?"

You pause by a classroom door and look through it and out the classroom windows. Except for a few puffy white clouds the sky is blue and some kids are outside with unzipped jackets and their hats and gloves stuffed into their pockets. "Okay, sure."

You and Rob go to your lockers and get your jackets. The memory of that day a week ago in the hall when he complimented you on your posters comes back. You recall the way he looked at you and start to wonder if it meant anything different than usual.

"Ready?" The nearness of his voice catches you by surprise. You spin around and there he is in a navy blue baseball jacket, the strap of his backpack slung over one shoulder, the computer bag now tucked under his arm. The jacket makes him look huskier than he really is.

And while you would not call him handsome, he is definitely cute.

You accidentally swing your locker door closed a little too hard. *Clang!* The sound is jarringly loud. Rob gives you a funny look. Together you leave school and start down the sidewalk. The air is cool, but not uncomfortable. The trees are dark and bare.

"Know what's so great about that skating rink idea?" he says. "We really don't need the whole rink anyway. And this way we won't have to pay for it."

"It wasn't my idea." The words just pop out, but you're not surprised. You've always been severely uncomfortable with lies. Sooner or later the truth always claws its way to the surface. "It was Tara's."

"But Celeste said—"

"She thinks it was my idea, too." Strangely, you don't mind admitting the truth to Rob. You know he's the kind of person who'll keep it to himself. As you walk together, the orange winter sun begins to drop toward the tree line and the chilly shadows grow long. You zip your jacket up to your chin and secretly wish you'd waited for the late bus.

"It doesn't really matter," goes Rob.

"It does to me."

"Well, it's brave of you to tell me," he says. It's his habit to always try to find something nice to say.

"I should have told everyone."

"Why?" Rob says. "You're smart, Lauren. You could have thought of it, too."

"Maybe." Now you begin to feel ashamed and embarrassed. Maybe you shouldn't have told him the truth. Not if you really do want him to like you.

As if he senses how uncomfortable you feel, he changes the subject. "So, did you check out what video games they have?"

"Sure, Rob, I tried out every one of them." You grin.

"Seriously."

"You can go check them out if you want. You don't have to wait for the party to do that."

"Aw, guess I'll wait." From there the conversation veers off into school and teachers and tests. Before long, you've reached the block where you both live. You stop on the sidewalk in front of your little house. The sun has dropped out of sight and with it the temperature. It's cold enough for your breath to come out in a small cloud of white.

"So, uh . . ." Rob scuffs his shoe against the sidewalk and seems uncertain of what to say. "See you tomorrow, okay?"

"You won't tell anyone, will you?" you ask.

He shakes his head. "Like I said, Lauren, as far as I'm concerned, you could have thought of it yourself."

"Thank you, Rob." You say this as softly and sweetly

as you can. Hoping he'll stay and say something. Something sincere that might indicate that he likes you more than just a friend.

"Well . . ." He pauses uncertainly. "See you tomorrow." He turns and heads toward his house.

Just friends, you think, feeling disappointed.

eighteen

"I'm coming to your house after school today," Celeste announces in the hall on the way to lunch the next day.

This catches you by surprise. Of course, you're delighted, but puzzled, too. "Well, great, but . . . why?"

"It's a surprise."

You feel a smile grow on your face, but it promptly vanishes when you and Celeste step into the cafeteria. Out in the land of the socially inferior, Tara is already sitting by herself at your regular table. Meanwhile, at the red-hot center of the social universe, the DYWYWM girls are crowded around theirs.

"You want to sit with Tara and me?" you ask Celeste.

"Oh, uh, I would, but I told Judy I'd plan decorations with her. Another time, okay?"

"Sure." You and she part ways. Everywhere else in school you're the co-treasurers and you almost feel like you are part of the A-list crowd. But here in the cafeteria, life is the way it's always been.

Later, Celeste takes the bus home with you. You are dying to know why she wants to come to your house, but she refuses to tell. This time there is no major chow down in the kitchen. She marches straight to your room and points at your vanity. "I want you there, now!"

"Why?" you giggle.

"Because it's time you got hip, girl." She takes a small makeup kit out of her bag. "Look what I got you."

It's a sample makeup kit. A week ago they were giving them away at JC Penney's.

"I don't need makeup," you protest.

"Oh, really? Every *other* girl on earth does. Why not you?"

"Because I'll never wear it."

"Tomorrow you will."

"Why?"

"Because it's dress-up day, remember?"

You'd totally forgotten. "Oh, okay. It's just that . . ."

"Just what?"

Just nothing except that you're still afraid people will think you're trying to be one of the DYWYWM girls. *"Can you believe Lauren? Just because she's co-treasurer she thinks she's suddenly popular."*

"Mom doesn't let me wear makeup," you lie. "Except on special occasions."

"Isn't dress-up day a special occasion?" Celeste asks

as she applies eye shadow over your eyes. "Besides, why does she have to know? First thing tomorrow morning, we'll do you up in the girls' room. And another thing. Tomorrow after school you're going to the bank."

"To get the money for the skating rink?"

"Uh . . ." In the mirror the lines between Celeste's eyes deepen. "No, we've got time for that."

"Then why?"

"Haven't you ever heard of robbers?" She points at the green ceramic barrel on your dresser. "What do you think would happen if a robber broke into this house and found that?"

"I—I guess he'd take it."

"Duh. So tomorrow after school you're putting it in the bank where it will be safe."

"I can do that?"

"Of course, silly, why not?"

"I thought you had to be a certain age."

"Nope. Anyone can open a bank account. And when you do, you'll get interest." One thing about Celeste: she's smart. Right away she picks up on your silence. "Okay, here's the deal on interest. When your money is in the bank, not only is it safe, but it grows."

"The nickels and dimes get bigger?" you joke.

"When you give your money to the bank, they add a little more each day. It's not a lot, but at least it's something. Suppose they give you five percent interest. On five hundred dollars that's twenty-five extra dollars a year."

How is it that Celeste is totally helpless in math class but can figure out how banking works? Probably because she doesn't care about math class. Anyway, twenty-five dollars for doing nothing sure beats a long night of baby-sitting.

"You'll come with me, won't you?" you ask.

"I would, but remember that doctor's appointment I messed up? Tomorrow's the day I really go."

"Suppose I wait till the day after and then you come with me?" you ask as she pats blush onto your cheeks.

"The day after is Saturday," Celeste says. "Serious, Laur, it's easy. You ask for Mr. Hansen and tell him you're from school. He'll help you do everything."

You know she's right. You're too old to have a piggy bank. There's still one big question in your mind, but it feels too dumb to ask. Only Celeste is so smart it's almost like she can read your thoughts. "Okay, Laur, now what?"

"Promise you won't laugh?" you ask.

"I'll try."

"Well, you know my mom works during the afternoons and evenings? So she can't take me. So . . . I'm not exactly sure how . . . I'm supposed to get the money to the bank."

Celeste scowls. "Come again."

"I can't see myself getting on the bus with *that*." You point at the piggy bank.

"Of course not. You put it in a bag or something." She goes over to your closet and starts to rummage through it. Not finding anything she likes, she puts her hands on her hips and looks around the room, tapping her foot. Finally, she focuses on your backpack. She picks it up and dumps out the books. "Here you go."

"You really think I can walk into the bank with a backpack filled with money?"

"Believe me, Laur, they'll take it any way they can get it." She drops your backpack on the floor and returns to the makeup table. "Now hold still, I'm going to try the mascara."

Celeste applies the mascara to your eyelashes. There is certainty and assurance in the way she handles the mascara stick. If there's one thing Celeste has a lot of, it's confidence. And gradually, as you spend more time with her, you are beginning to feel more confident, too. When you are around her, it just seems to go on like makeup.

"Ta-da!" She steps back and you see yourself in the mirror. Once again you look like you're twenty-five years old.

"What do you think?" she asks proudly.

You stare at the person in the mirror. It's weird how much older you look, but fun and exciting, too. It would be so cool if you could really be that person. Maybe Celeste is right. For dress-up day tomorrow you can. And Rob will see you. Celeste puts a CD on the boom box and pulls some blank sheets of paper off your desk. "Let's draw."

"Uh, okay." Another thing about Celeste—she's full of surprises. *Draw?* You've never seen her even doodle in her notebook. Still, a few moments later you two lay side by side on your stomachs on the floor with pencils, drawing and gossiping.

"Remember when Judy kidded Krista about a boy named Peter coming to the skating party?" Celeste goes. "I found out he used to be Krista's boyfriend . . . until he dumped her."

You feel your jaw fall. "Krista Rice has been dumped?"

"Hard to believe, right?"

"Try impossible."

"He goes to Portswell across town. They went together almost all of last year. Judy doesn't know why he dumped her, but Krista goes ballistic when anyone brings him up."

"Except Judy," you point out.

"There's not much Krista can do about that."

"What do you mean?"

Celeste leans close. "When Judy and I work on decorations for the party we talk about the way Krista tries to control everything. Keep everyone in their place, you know? Judy would love to see Krista get knocked down a few rungs. And to tell you the truth, so would I."

You are fascinated and thrilled. This is it! The secrets you've been dying to hear. The inside story. The juicy tidbits the A-list girls share only with one another. Celeste seems lost in thought for a moment.

"Know what?" she suddenly says. "You're right. It'll look really dumb if you walk into the bank and just dump a backpack full of money on a desk. They might even think *you* were a robber."

Huh? How did she go from secrets about Krista's love life back to money so fast? Who cares about the money? You want to hear more secrets.

"I think you should organize it," Celeste decides. "Like put all the bills in order and put all the coins in rolls."

"Rolls?"

"You know. The paper tubes the lunch ladies are always banging open into the cash registers."

"Oh, right."

"I'll get some for you tomorrow. Now let's practice our signatures."

"Why?"

"It's fun. Haven't you ever done it?"

"No."

"Look." Celeste signs her name once with regular-size letters and once with big loopy letters. "This is how I normally do it. But maybe I should do it this way. What do you think?"

You point at the loopy signature. "That looks like the way a movie star would do it."

"Cool. We're going to Hollywood, remember? Now how about yours?"

You sign your name the normal way, then try it with big loopy letters, too. You both spend another half an hour practicing different ways of signing your names. Meanwhile, Celeste tells you how the A-list girls really can't stand Stephanie, but they tolerate her not just because her dad throws those parties at Carmen's, but because Stephanie's house has a pool and a hot tub that are total boy magnets in the summer.

"I feel kind of bad for her," Celeste says. "I mean, deep inside she has to know."

Then it's time for Celeste to go. Once again she doesn't have money for a cab, but you don't mind lending her some. It's just so much fun having her around.

nineteen

"Mom, I can't wear this scarf to school."

"Come on, hon, have some fun. You could wear this pearl necklace doubled over like a choker. And let's try a little makeup."

"I can't, Mom."

"But it's dress-up day."

"Why did I open my big mouth and tell you?"

"I honestly don't understand you, Lauren. Who'll care?"

"The other girls."

"But they'll all be dressed up, too."

"I know. I'm sorry, Mom. I can't explain it."

In typical Lauren Walsh style you leave for school dressed as Ms. Totally Plain in your nicest skirt, blouse, and sweater. You're dressed up—for church. What happened to the confidence you felt yesterday? It seems to have left with Celeste. Half the kids at the bus stop are dressed up. A few have decided that *dress up* means "dress crazy." Rob shows up wearing a tie and jacket . . .

and a white clown face with a red nose and a bright orange clown wig.

"You look nice, Lauren," he says.

"Thanks, Rob. You look . . ." You almost say "ridiculous," but catch yourself just in time. "Uh, funny."

He grins. "Hey, I'm dressed up, aren't I?"

It's hard to believe that Rob, who is usually so reserved and preppy, would do something so outrageous. Isn't he worried about calling attention to himself? Doesn't it bother him that people might laugh at him?

Yours is the first stop so the bus is always empty when you get on. You settle into your seat and glance out the window to see if any late kids are running down the block.

"May I join you?" Clown Rob is standing in the aisle.

"Sure." You are, of course, surprised. He's never sat with you before.

"So let me guess," he says after he slides into the seat beside you. "You're supposed to be, uh . . . not a business woman. Not a college student . . . I know! A spy."

"How'd you guess?"

"Couldn't think of anything else."

The bus begins to bump along. You think of something and smile.

"What's so funny?" he asks.

"When I saw you dressed like that, I wondered why you weren't afraid that kids would laugh at you. Then I realized you're dressed like a clown! People are *supposed* to laugh at you."

"Like, duh."

"I know. It's just . . . Oh, forget it."

At the next stop more kids get on, including Shelby Kirk, a long-time member of the DYWYWM crowd, and the girl Rob defeated for class secretary. Shelby has bright red hair and blue eyes that lock on you and Rob sitting together. You feel yourself begin to blush, then realize Rob is looking at you, too.

"Seriously, Lauren," he says in a low voice, "why do you care so much about what other people think?"

You just shrug. "Don't *you* care?"

"Not really."

"Then why'd you run for class secretary?"

Rob's red clown lips widen until you see his small white teeth. "Because if you want to get a scholarship to a good college, it really helps to show that you're a well-rounded student who held an office in student government in high school. And if you want to get elected in high school, it helps to show you did a good job in middle school."

"So it's all about getting a college scholarship?" you ask.

"It's that or community college."

Hardly anyone you know really thinks much about college yet. But even at Woodville Middle School everyone knows the local community college is a joke unless you plan to be a computer technician, electrician, or beautician. Anyway, as far as caring what people think about you, maybe it's just that Rob is a boy and boys don't worry as much about things like that.

At school you expect Celeste to be waiting at your locker. So you're disappointed when she isn't there. You even dawdle in the hallway longer than usual, hoping that she will show up, but she doesn't. Finally, you go down the hall and peek into her homeroom, but she isn't there, either. That leaves only one other place—the girls' room.

You place a trembling hand against the girls' room door and push. Inside it's just as you imagined. In the perfumed mist the A-list girls are lined up at the mirrors, dressed in their fanciest clothes, busy fixing their makeup, and primping their hair. Right in the middle is Celeste, wearing the black low-cut top you loaned her and a black satin choker with a single pearl in the center.

As soon as they hear the door hinges squeak, everyone looks in your direction. An icy chill of fear freezes you, but no one frowns or wrinkles her nose. Most just go back to their makeup and hair.

Except Celeste, who winks first, *then* goes back to her hair.

Briiinnnggg! The bell rings and the girls' room starts to clear out. You leave with Celeste.

"We never got to do your makeup," she says as you walk together quickly down the hall to your homerooms.

"It's okay."

"You sure?" she asks.

"Totally."

"Oh, here." She digs into her bag and pulls out a handful of paper tubes for coins. They are all white, but some have thin green stripes, others red or yellow stripes. And they're different widths for different-size coins. "Looks like you'll be having fun this weekend."

"Yeah, right." You groan at the thought of counting all your coins and stuffing them into rolls.

"Doing any baby-sitting?"

"Three jobs. Tonight, tomorrow night, and Sunday afternoon."

"Busy girl. Okay, catch you later." She veers off. You're secretly relieved that she didn't insist on making you up. But you also wish she would have tried harder.

twenty

"You hear about Reed and Krista?" Tara asks at lunch.

You could have worn makeup. You could have dressed much cooler. After the way they all accepted you in the girls' room, you feel more certain than ever that you could be sitting at the DYWYWM table right now, wearing makeup because it's dress-up day, and sharing A-list gossip and secrets.

"Hello?" goes Tara. "Yoo-hoo. Earth to Lauren."

"Huh?"

"I asked if you heard about Reed and Krista."

"What about them?"

"I don't understand, Lauren. Now that you're popular, I thought you knew about *everything*."

"Give it a rest, Tara. What's the story?"

Chewing on one of her beef jerkies, Tara leans close. "Reed asked Jason to ask Stephanie if Krista would skate with him at the skating party."

"Oh, that."

Tara eyes you. "You *knew*?"

"Everybody knows Reed and Krista like each other."

"Oh, excu-u-use me." Tara crosses her arms and pretends to pout. "I thought it was fresh gossip."

Sometimes her sarcasm can be really annoying. It may be dress-up day, but she's wearing old jeans that are rubbed shiny on the thighs, and the white sweatshirt with the washed-out stains.

You finish lunch in silence. Celeste and some of the other A-list girls get up and go outside. Through the cafeteria windows you see that the sky is blue except for a few powder-puff clouds. Boys in shirtsleeves are throwing a football around. Girls in sweaters and unzipped jackets stand in groups talking. It's another unusually warm and sunny day for this time of year.

"Looks nice outside." You stand up.

Tara glances out the window and sees Celeste and the others. Then she gazes up at you. "Lauren?"

You freeze, expecting more sarcasm. "Yes?"

"You look nice."

"Thanks, Tara." The stress drains out of you. Tara's your friend. She wouldn't hurt your feelings on purpose. Maybe she told you that stuff about Krista and Reed because she wants to be in the crowd, too. Maybe she's simply afraid of losing you.

Outside, you spot Celeste standing beside a big tree with her back to you. The trunk is so wide that three kids can easily fit around it with their arms spread. When you're close enough to reach out and touch her, you realize she's talking to someone on the other side of the tree.

"You can't tell anyone I told you this," she's saying in a low voice. "But Krista's really hoping her old boyfriend, Peter, will skate with her."

"Peter Sandifer?" That's Jason Buckley's voice. "He goes to Portswell."

"That doesn't mean he can't come to the skating party," Celeste goes. "And I hear he's a really good skater."

"Yeah, he is," Jason says. "They skate against us in hockey. Think I should warn Reed?"

"I don't know," Celeste says. "I'm just telling you what I heard."

"I better let Reed know." Jason makes up his mind.

"Make sure you tell him it's only a rumor," goes Celeste. "I mean, even if it's true, just because Krista's *hoping* Peter will come doesn't mean he will."

"I know," Jason says. "But Reed would still want to know."

As he starts to come around the tree you duck around the other side. "Celeste?"

She turns, and looks surprised. "Oh, hi, Laur. What's up?"

"I heard what you just said to Jason. Didn't Krista say

that she never wants to talk to Peter again for as long as she lives?"

Celeste lowers her forehead and her eyes almost disappear behind her bangs. "Okay, I'm going to tell you something you can't tell anyone else, understand?"

"Yes."

"You're right. Krista's not waiting for Peter to ask her to the skating party. She's waiting for Reed to ask her."

"But you told Jason—"

"Wouldn't it be nice if just for once Krista didn't get what she wanted?" Celeste cuts in. "Wouldn't it be totally great if she got to the skating party and didn't have anyone to skate with?"

You don't know what to say. You're stunned that Celeste made up the story about Krista wanting Peter to take her to the skating party. Celeste puts her hands on her hips and leans toward you, dropping her voice. "Judy feels the same way I do. And so do a lot of the other girls. Only they're afraid to say so. Don't you get it, Laur? I did it for *you*. Aren't you tired of Krista deciding who's in and who's out? Don't you think it's time someone knocked her off her throne?"

"Yes, but—"

"Aren't you sick of her deciding who sits at *her* table? Like she owns it? I mean, who gave Krista Rice the right to rule the rest of us?"

It's as if she's read your innermost thoughts.

"It could be totally different, Laur. And not just for you. For everyone. Even Tara. Wouldn't it be great if we were all equal? If we all sat wherever we wanted and had whatever friends we wanted? If we completely got rid of all the stupid cliquey garbage?"

"But . . . *you're* popular."

"So?" Celeste frowns as if she doesn't understand. Then she gets it. "Oh, Laur, I like everyone. I don't care who's popular and who isn't. What I care about is that everyone is equal. Wouldn't that be great?"

"Absolutely."

"Well, that's what's going to happen. But *only* if you can keep a secret."

Now you understand. "And you want it to happen at the skating party because the whole grade will be there?"

"Can you think of a better place?" Celeste asks, smiling.

twenty-one

"So the skating party is next Friday, hon?"

"I can't wait."

"You should be proud. It was your idea and you made it happen. Is Tara going?"

"Probably not, Mom. She doesn't skate."

"But she's your best friend. And not everyone who goes skates, do they?"

"No."

"Don't you think you should see if you can get her to go?"

You spend the weekend baby-sitting, sorting and counting coins, and flattening out bills. At school on Monday you see Celeste.

"Ready to go to the bank after school?" she asks.

"Sure am . . . Only, don't banks close at three?"

"First National is open till five on Mondays. Also, I've been thinking. You know all those rolls of coins?"

"Do I ever." You groan at the memory of sorting, counting, and sealing them.

"You're probably better off turning them in to a teller first and getting bills. It'll just make everything easier."

"What would make it easier is if you came with me."

"Can't. Doctor's appointment, remember?"

"I thought you said it was Friday."

"Oh, right. I meant dentist."

At home after school you put the bills and rolls of coins into your backpack and climb on your bike. It feels so strange. On your bike you must look like any other kid with a backpack, but you're scared. What if some robber has X-ray vision and can see into your pack? What if you fall and all the money spills out? If only Celeste were with you.

Of course you ride all the way without being robbed or falling down. You get to the bank just as a blue-and-yellow town bus pulls away from a bus stop in front. Glancing in the windows you thought you caught a glimpse of maroon knit cap just like Celeste's.

A moment later, the bus is halfway down the block and you begin to wonder if you just have a bad case of Celeste on the brain.

Inside, the bank is set up like some kind of techno living room. To your left, a row of tellers sits behind a counter, but there are no Plexiglas windows to separate them from the public. In the center are some comfortable-looking gray chairs, a large television, and a few children's toys on an orange-and-pink rug on the floor. The bank officers sit at curving gray desks to the right.

Following Celeste's instructions, you go up to one of the tellers and turn in all the rolls of coins for bills. Then you go over to the desks where the officers sit.

A red-haired woman in a navy blue suit looks up from her desk. "Can I help you?"

"I'm here to see Mr. Hansen."

The woman turns her head toward another desk where a man with short gray hair sits speaking to another man who is mostly bald. Both wear dark suits, white shirts, and ties. The man with the short gray hair has bushy black eyebrows. "He's speaking to someone right now," the red-haired woman reports. "Please have a seat."

You sit down on one of the cushiony gray chairs. On the TV a woman is talking about the stock market. Charts and graphs fill the space behind her, and rows of mysterious letters and numbers crawl across the screen beneath her. It amazes you that there are television channels devoted twenty-four hours a day to money. Who could possibly care that much?

Back at the desk, both men rise and shake hands. The bald man leaves and the gray-haired man turns to you. "Can I help you?" He gestures to the chair where the bald man was just sitting and smiles reassuringly. "Please, have a seat. I'm Jay Hansen. Your name is?" He extends his hand.

"Lauren Walsh." You shake his hand.

"Pleased to meet you, Lauren."

You sit down. The seat feels warm. "Well, I go to Woodville and—"

"Oh, yes. Carol told me you'd be coming in. The new school treasurer."

"Right. Anyway I want to put some money in the bank."

"Excellent. Is this your first time here?"

You nod.

"Well, it's very simple." Mr. Hansen pulls open a desk drawer and takes out a slip of paper. "We'll fill out this deposit slip and then you'll take it over to the teller." He turns to his computer and begins to type. "Now let's see the number on the class account."

"It's not for the class account."

Mr. Hansen stops typing. "Sorry?"

"I want to start my own account."

"Oh." He smiles. "We can do that, too." He opens his desk drawer again and takes out a letter-size form, then tells you about the kinds of savings accounts you can have. You pick the one that sounds the best, and then sign the form. Once again he reaches for the deposit slip. "And how much would you like to deposit?"

"Four hundred and twenty-eight dollars."

Mr. Hansen's eyes widen and his black eyebrows rise. "Wow, that's a lot for a young lady like you."

"It's from years of baby-sitting." You open your back-pack and take out the neatly stacked bills.

"You must be one very busy young lady."

"I guess."

"Well, it's good. Someday there'll be something you'll really want and you'll be glad you saved."

It's funny that he says that. You know what you want, but it's not something money can buy.

twenty-two

"It's late. Shouldn't you go to bed?"

"Soon as I finish, Mom."

"More posters?"

"For the skating party."

"Hon, isn't this last year's Spanish book?"

"Oh, yeah. My friend Celeste left it here by accident."

"This homework has her name, but it looks like your handwriting."

"Oh, I, er, just helped her with it."

"You're sure you didn't do it for her?"

"Mom!"

Four days until the skating party. Halfway through English, the last period of the day, the loudspeaker crackles. "Lauren Walsh and Celeste Van Warner, please come to the office right away."

Everyone stares at you. It's unusual for Principal Hansen to call kids down to her office in the middle of class. Out in the hall you see Celeste step out of a classroom a few doors down.

"What's going on?" you ask.

"You got me." Celeste shrugs, then starts to bite one of her fingernails. "Probably something to do with the skating party. Have you decided if you're going to wear your skating outfit?"

"I still can't decide." Together you start down the hall.

"I really think you'll look great in it, Laur."

"You don't think it'll look a little corny?" you ask. "I just know everyone else will be wearing jeans and sweaters."

"It'll make you look unique," Celeste answers. "Besides, when they see how good you skate they'll understand."

"Thanks, you always know how to make me feel good."

Celeste laughs. "Believe me, Laur, you're easy."

You get to the main office.

"Go right in, girls." The secretary points at the door to Principal Hansen's private office. Inside, Principal Hansen is sitting at her desk, a pen in one hand, looking down at some papers. Two buttons on her phone blink, but she hasn't taken either call. She looks up. "Have a seat, girls."

No smile. No "hello." Celeste gives you a puzzled glance as you both sit down in the chairs facing the desk.

"I just received a call from Dick Johnson, the owner of the skating rink," Principal Hansen says. "Are you aware that he hasn't gotten the money for the party yet?"

"We're going to the bank today to get the money," Celeste says.

Principal Hansen cups her hands on the desk in front of her. "I'm confused, girls. According to my husband, you closed the class account a week ago Monday."

"Closed the account? What does that mean?" Celeste asks.

Principal Hansen raises a carefully tweezed eyebrow. "When you close an account, it means you take out all the money."

"But—we didn't," you sputter.

"I didn't," says Celeste.

Principal Hansen's thin crescent eyebrows dip in toward each other. "Well, someone did. And without that money you can't pay the skating rink and there can't be a skating party."

A fog of numb shock envelops you. Something's wrong.

"Can't we find out who took the money?" Celeste asks.

"We'll have to," Principal Hansen replies. "Until now I assumed it was you two, but you say you didn't."

A flashing red warning light slashes through the fog around you. It's something in her voice. Something that suspects this isn't just about some missing money.

"Both of you go back to class," Principal Hansen says. "I'll let you know if I find out anything else."

Back out in the hall, Celeste says, "I don't get it."

"Neither do I," you agree. "I hope it's just the bank's mistake. I remember my mom once saying they accidentally put a bunch of money that belonged to someone else in her account."

"It *better* be the bank's mistake," Celeste says grimly. "Because you know what's going to happen if they can't find that money?"

"You don't think we'd *really* have to cancel the party, do you?"

"What choice would we have?" Celeste answers. "If there's no money, we can't rent the skating rink."

twenty-three

The next morning you go straight to the office when school starts. Principal Hansen is standing at the counter reading through some papers. When she looks up and sees you, her eyebrows tilt down and almost touch. Like a bird with wide, arcing wings.

"Did you find out about the money?" you ask.

"It's not even nine o'clock, Lauren. The bank hasn't opened yet."

"Oh." You didn't think of that.

"Get along to your class," Principal Hansen says.

"Would you tell me as soon as you hear anything?" you beg.

"Yes, Lauren, I certainly will."

For the next few periods, you can't concentrate in class. All you can think about is how the party just can't be canceled. Now that you know Celeste's plan, it has to happen! And not just for you, but also for everyone who's ever been scorned by Krista and the other A-list girls.

No matter where your next class is, you make a point of going past the office in the hope that Principal Hansen will see you and have some news. She sees you twice, but both times just gives you a funny scowl and shakes her head.

Right before lunch Principal Hansen's expression changes. When she sees you in the hall she waves you into the office.

"Let's go into my room," she says, gesturing down the short narrow hall inside the main office. You go in and sit in the same chair you sat in the day before. Principal Hansen sits down on the other side of the desk. Interlacing her fingers, she leans forward on both elbows. "My husband just called. He found the withdrawal slip that was used to close the account. It has both your name and Celeste's on it."

"That's not possible!" you gasp. "I didn't sign any withdrawal slips and Celeste couldn't have done it without me."

"There's always the unfortunate possibility that someone forged your signatures," Principal Hansen says.

"But if they did that and took the money, it's not our fault."

"The money's still gone, Lauren. And without it, Mr. Johnson won't let you have the party."

From Principal Hansen's office you go straight to the cafeteria. It's lunchtime now and Celeste is sitting at the

DYWYWM table, chatting happily with the other girls as if she doesn't have a care in the world. You touch her on the shoulder and whisper in her ear. "We have to talk."

The conversation stops. Everyone looks at you. You feel a shiver of self-consciousness and wish you weren't doing this. But what's really strange is that you are doing it—standing right there in front of all the A-list girls, and interrupting them. And that's something you never could have done before.

"Talk about what?" Celeste asks.

"You *know*."

Celeste makes sure everyone sees her frown as she gets up. Why is she acting as if she has no idea what this is about? You both step away from the table to get some privacy.

"You won't believe this," you whisper. "Principal Hansen spoke to her husband. Someone forged our names on the withdrawal slip and took the money."

Celeste puts her hand on your shoulder. "Oh, Laur, that's totally not fair."

Tears unexpectedly flood into your eyes, and you quickly turn away and start out of the cafeteria. The last thing in the world you want is to let the A-list table see you cry. On the way past the land of the socially inferior, you catch a glimpse of Tara sitting alone at your usual table. She gives you a concerned look and places her hands flat on the table, as if to get up. You shake your head and gesture for her not to follow. Out in the hallway you lean against a cold tile wall, press your face into your hands, and let the tears spill out.

Celeste comes out into the hall. "Laur?"

"It's not fair," you sob, wiping the tears from your cheeks.

She gives you a hug. "You're right. It was going to be your night. More than anyone else's, your star was going to shine."

"I'll do anything to go to that party. *Anything!*"

"But there's nothing you can do . . . unless you want to pay for it yourself."

You pull back and stare at her through watery eyes. She's right! It would be that easy! "Then that's what we'll do," you announce, straightening up with determination. "I've got the money in my account. We'll use it to pay for the party."

Celeste raises her hands as if to stop you. "Wait, Laur, I wasn't serious. There's no way you're going to use the money you worked so hard for to pay for the stupid skating party."

"All I'll do is *lend* the money," you explain. "Then, when this whole thing is straightened out, I'll get it back." You grab her hand and pull. "Come on, let's go tell Principal Hansen that's what we're going to do."

"Whoa." Celeste pulls back and doesn't budge. "I don't know if I want to go see her so fast, Laur. I kind of feel like a jerk. I mean, we took this job and she gave us that lecture about responsibility and the first thing we did was blow it big time."

"But it's not our fault."

"I know, but . . . look, let's think for a second. Who else do we know? I mean, maybe someone whose parents would have the money."

"Krista?"

"Oh, right." Celeste rolls her eyes. "We get her to put up the money and then she goes to the party and we shoot her down. That's really nice."

"What about Stephanie?"

"I couldn't ask her," Celeste says. "Could you?"

"No. What about your parents?"

"Forget it. I'm already in trouble for the credit-card bill I ran up this month. What about your mom?"

"No way."

Celeste crosses her arms and gazes off down the hall. "There has to be someone."

"There is. Me. And I just remembered something else Principal Hansen said. Mr. Johnson has to have the money *tomorrow*. Face it, Celeste. We don't have the time to figure out where else to get the money. I have it, and all we have to do is go to the bank after school and take it out of my account and give it to him."

Celeste places her hands on your shoulders again, and looks straight into your eyes. "Know what, Laur? You are a really good person to even *volunteer* to do that. An *incredibly* good person. But I still don't want you to do it. Let's wait and think. I bet before school is over we'll come up with another way to save the party."

"Don't be so sure," you warn her.

"Let's just think about it, okay?" she asks. "We'll meet at your locker at the end of school and see if we haven't come up with a better idea."

"Sure," you answer. "Whatever."

twenty-four

At the end of school you meet Celeste at your locker. "Think of anything?"

She purses her lips and shakes her head, frustrated. "Have you?"

"The only thing I can think of is using my money. Really, Celeste, it's okay. I'm sure the bank will find the school's money, and when they do, we'll just pay me back with it."

"I still don't like it," she argues.

"Look, Celeste, I really don't want the skating party to get canceled, okay? It's really, really important to me. So you're just going to do this with me and not argue." It's hard to believe that you spoke those words so firmly and with such assurance. But for once you are sure, and completely confident that you're doing the right thing.

Celeste hesitates. She's still unsure. Somehow that makes you feel even more certain that this is the right thing to do. "Come on, we have to go to the bank." You take her hand. "Now."

But she pulls her hand out of yours. "I can't, Laur. I promised my mom I'd help her with some Christmas shopping."

"Why don't you call her and tell her to meet us at the mall after we drop the money off at the skating rink?"

"Uh, she wants to go someplace else." Celeste seems suddenly distracted. Her eyes dart this way and that and you sense she's thinking about other things.

"You okay?" you ask.

"Huh? Oh, yeah."

"What about tomorrow?" you ask.

"We're going to go shopping tomorrow, too," she answers. She wants to leave. You know you should let her, but it's hard to let go.

"Want to come over after school on Friday and help me get ready for the party?" you ask.

"Yeah, definitely," Celeste says. "Let's do that."

"Great, see you then." You watch her go off down the hall, and then you head for the bank. You get there just before closing time and withdraw the three hundred dollars out of your account. From there you go to the skating rink and give it to Mr. Johnson.

There. It's done, and you did it all by yourself. Outside the skating rink, the afternoon sky is graying toward evening, and people are bundled in coats, hats, and scarves. The wind has picked up and their scarves flap behind them as they walk. A white paper cup skitters along the road. You feel so good you decide to walk home despite the cold and the wind and the approaching darkness. Nothing's going to stop the skating party now.

twenty-five

For the past few weeks you have bought a school lunch every day. It is costly, considering it means pitching the lunch your mother makes for you and then paying for the new lunch yourself. But it's worth it. Only today there's no point in buying a whole lunch. You barely have an appetite. Tonight is the skating party and you're so excited you could get away without eating anything. But you get in line for some fries just because you're afraid you'll be hungry later.

Someone taps you on the shoulder and you turn to find Krista and Rob.

"Everything ready for tonight?" Krista asks.

"Oh, yeah." You feel a strange pang of guilt. Krista was once your friend and now you are planning to do something mean to her. Even if she'd never been your friend, is it ever right to be mean to anyone?

"Can't wait to check out those video games," Rob chimes in.

You force a smile on your face and move closer to the food counter.

"You've done a great job, Lauren," Krista says, then lowers her voice. "And everyone knows you did most of the work."

"Oh, that's not true," you answer. "Just wait till you see the decorations."

Krista doesn't say anything. You go up to the counter and get your fries. "Well, see you later."

"Wait, Lauren," Krista says. "Why don't you ever sit with us?"

You know you heard her clearly, but you still can't believe your ears. "Oh, well, I'd love to, but, you know—" You tilt your head toward the land of the socially inferior— "Tara."

"She can sit with us, too," Krista goes.

This results in temporary brain freeze. You're totally not sure what to make of it. It is so out of the blue. So not the way you thought things were. You look over at the DYWYWM table. It is already crowded with girls. Celeste and Judy are shoulder to shoulder, their heads tilted toward each other, talking. "Doesn't look like there's room."

Krista nods. "But another time, okay?"

"Sure. Thanks."

On dazed autopilot you head for the table where

Tara sits. What just happened? What does it mean? Is it possible that Krista knows Celeste is up to something and is being nice to you to find out what it is? Or, is it possible that Krista is just plain being nice?

"What did Krista want?" Tara asks as you join her.

"Just making sure everything's ready for tonight."

"Bet you'll get brownie points for this," Tara quips.

You force a weak smile. Suddenly you're uncertain. Now that Krista's being nice to you, you don't know what you'll get. "Sure you don't want to come tonight?" Given how confused you are, it would be nice if Tara were around to help you think straight.

"Thanks, but I'd rather watch dust balls grow under my couch."

Lunch ends and you really need to speak to Celeste, but she leaves the cafeteria still talking to Judy. As the day continues, you look for her in the hall between classes. Finally, when school ends, you wait for her at her locker. You spot her with Judy, but the hall is crowded and they don't see you yet.

"I'll go home and get the streamers and tablecloths," Judy's saying. "When's your mom taking you to get the balloons?"

"Soon as I get home," Celeste replies.

Not expecting to hear this, you blurt, "Celeste?"

She looks up, surprised to see you. "Oh, hey, Laur."

"I thought. . ." You don't want to continue while Judy's there.

Celeste gives you a puzzled look. Then her jaw drops as if she's just remembered why you're waiting by her locker. "Oh, uh, I just have a couple of things to do first for the party. So I'll come over to your house later, okay?"

"Okay." You're a little disappointed, but you wouldn't say anything in front of Judy. Meanwhile, the pace in the hall begins to pick up as kids head toward the bus circle.

"Lauren, I hear you're a really good skater," Judy says with a sincere smile.

"I'm okay."

"Guess we'll see tonight," she says.

"I guess."

"Oh, Judy, there's something else I forgot." Celeste pulls the focus back to herself. It's odd, the way she needs Judy's full attention, but you don't have time to dwell on it. Lockers are slamming shut and kids are starting to run. If you don't hurry, you're going to miss your bus.

"See you later!" you call to Celeste as you start down the hall. If she answers you, you don't hear it.

chapter
twenty-six

"Aren't you late for the party, hon?"

"I guess."

"Who do you keep trying to call? What's wrong?"

"Nothing, Mom."

"Come on, hon. You should be excited. This is your big night. Do you know what you want to wear?"

"The turquoise outfit."

"I have some eye shadow that would go great with it."

"I don't know, Mom."

"Come on, I see all the girls your age wearing makeup. You don't have to wear a lot. Just enough to bring out your features. This would be the perfect night for it."

"Oh, okay."

"That a girl."

You're almost finished getting ready when the phone rings. You quickly reach for the receiver. *It must be Celeste calling to explain why she couldn't come to your house to help you get ready.*

"Hello?"

"Hey." It's Tara.

"Oh, hi."

"Who were you expecting to call?" She's so quick.

"Doesn't matter."

"Getting ready?"

"Trying. I'm already late."

"What time does it start?"

"Like fifteen minutes ago. Why? Are you thinking about going?"

"Dream on."

"Then?"

"I just wanted to wish you good luck. I hope you have a good time tonight."

"Oh, Tara, you're so sweet. Seriously, why don't you come?"

"And miss a rerun of *Star Trek: Insurrection*? Have you lost your mind?"

"I guess."

"I want a full report, okay?"

"On what?" you ask. "I thought you didn't care."

"Oh, yeah. Almost forgot. So just let me know how it goes, okay? For you."

"You got it." You hang up.

"Ready, hon?" Mom calls from the front door.

"Just a second!" You hurry back to your room to get your skates. The light is off and when you switch it on, you catch your reflection in the makeup table mirror—a girl in a turquoise skating outfit, her hair in a French braid, a touch of makeup. You stand motionless, knowing you'll be the only girl at the party tonight in an outfit like this. The rest of the kids will be wearing jeans and sweaters. Suddenly you feel an intense urge to get out of this costume and into clothes that will make you look like everyone else. Clothes that will let you blend in and be like everyone else. You know this urge is driven by fear. Fear that you will walk into the party and people will point at you behind your back and say mean things. You reach behind your neck and start to unzip the outfit.

Then you stop.

Why do you have to be like everyone else?

Why do you have to look like everyone else?

That's all you've been doing for years, and it hasn't changed a thing. What makes you think you're so important that anyone would even care what you wore? And so what if they say mean things behind your back? You don't have to wear this skating outfit to get them to do that. And why would you want mean girls for friends anyway? Tara may be heavy, and she may wear yucky clothes, but she's a good person and close friend and she's not afraid to say nice things.

"Hon?" your mom calls through the house. "By the time you get there you'll be half an hour late."

You go to your closet and get the skates, but on the way out you stop and look at the girl in the mirror again. You feel a smile creep onto your lips. Suppose they do point? Suppose they do say mean things behind your back? At least they'll notice you.

twenty-seven

You get to the ice rink and hurry into the concession and rental room. The tangy aroma of hot dogs mixes with the heavy scent of damp wool. Ice-skate blades click against the floor as groups of chattering kids bang through the swinging doors from the ice rink and head for the food stand. *Whizz-bang!* sounds burst from the video games lining the hall just past the rental stand. Rob is bent over one of the machines, his face illuminated by the yellows, reds, and blues flashing off the screen. You're tempted to go say hello, to let him see you wearing makeup and your turquoise skating outfit, but the pull of the scene out on the ice is much greater right now. You sit down on a wooden bench and start to lace up your skates. You're dying to see if Celeste's "plot" has worked.

Before you finish lacing, the double doors to the ice rink swing open and Krista clamps through on her skates. She's wearing the most adorable pink-and-white snowflake Polartec jacket, jeans, and white skates that look so new you suspect she bought them just for this party. But her face is blotched red and streaked with tears as she heads directly for the girls' room. The ice rink doors swing open again and Stephanie Eisley follows, walking on her skates. Not crying herself. Definitely following Krista to lend support. You're sure neither of them noticed you.

This can only mean one thing: *Celeste's plan worked!* The DYWYWM crowd has been torn apart! You race to lace up the other skate, impatient that your fingers can't move any faster. Then you're up on your feet, clumping as fast as you can toward the swinging doors.

You push through. The loud music invades your ears and that first blast of cold air slaps your face. The left side of the rink is all little kids and parents, but on the other side of the bright orange cones is your grade. Skating in a slow circle around the perimeter, laughing, falling, standing around in groups on the inside ice, gabbing.

You eagerly look around for Celeste and spot her out on the ice. The sight stops you cold. Celeste is wearing the most gorgeous and sexy pink skating outfit with spaghetti straps, a handkerchief front skirt, mesh midriff, and flesh-colored tights. Where did she get that outfit? How? Why is she wearing it?

It takes a moment to shake off your surprise. Then you get it. Celeste is wearing that outfit so that you won't be the only one in a skating dress. It's her way of making sure you won't be singled out and scorned.

You feel a wave of warm relief, and a smile creeps onto your face. Celeste is standing on the ice with Shelby Kirk. From the way Celeste's ankles bend in and her knees wobble and she holds out her hands for balance, you can see that she's hardly ever been on skates before.

You step onto the ice and glide effortlessly. Skating to you is as natural as breathing. You head toward Celeste and Shelby.

But before you reach them, Reed Palmer and Jason Buckley cut across the ice and get there first. Jason stops beside Shelby, and Reed circles around behind Celeste, taking her by the elbow to help steady her. You feel a strange chill. It's the unexpectedly relaxed way that Reed holds Celeste's arm, and the way she allows him. As if this isn't the first time they've touched. Or even the sixth.

Something tells you to make a quick detour into the crowd of slowly circling skaters. You weave through the crowd and watch the two couples on the middle ice. Even with Reed there for support, Celeste can hardly keep her skates from sliding out from beneath her. Reed is busy trying to keep her from falling. Laughing and crying out in fake fear, she throws an arm around his neck and hangs on to him.

No wonder Krista ran into the girls' room crying.

The four of them stay in the middle of the ice and talk and laugh as if they're the only ones there. As if it's the DYWYWM table moved to the rink. You repeatedly catch Celeste's eye, but she only looks away and doesn't wave. Why is she ignoring you?

Finally, you give up and get off the ice. You stand by the skating rink rail feeling miserable and confused. Is Celeste so swept away by Reed that she's forgotten the plan? Or has she been plotting this all along? You can't help thinking back to that day by the big tree, overhearing her tell that lie to Jason about Krista wanting Peter Sandifer to come to the skating party.

Out on the ice the two couples begin to skate. Celeste with Reed practically holding her up. Shelby and Jason. As they join the counterclockwise flow of skaters, they pass the rail where you're standing. You give Celeste a little wave. She looks away and smiles warmly at Reed.

You feel a heavy sensation on your shoulders. Sadness. Anger. Regret. It's obvious now, isn't it? You were fooled. It was never about everyone becoming equal. It was only about Celeste replacing Krista as queen of the DYWYWM girls. Oddly, you're not taken entirely by surprise. It's as if somewhere deep inside you had a feeling this might be the case. The lies Celeste told. Her not showing up at your house earlier tonight. You just didn't want to see the signs. Now you have no choice.

The four of them circle around and pass you again. Celeste still refuses to look in your direction, and you start to feel useless and silly just standing there by the rail. You're dying to go out and skate, but you don't want to skate alone.

The endless circle of kids in pairs, threesomes, and quartets skates past you. The music plays amid laughter and shouts. Everyone seems happy, and despite the hurt of Celeste's betrayal, you do feel an unexpected sense of pride and accomplishment. The party was your idea, and thanks to you it has happened.

The kids who aren't skating sit on benches or walk around outside the rail. Out of the corner of your eye you see Rob with a group of his friends. He glances in your direction. You smile and he smiles back. You turn and look back at the skaters again, praying hard that he'll decide to come over and talk.

Nothing happens. After a few more moments, you look in his direction again, but he and his friends have gone. You let out a deep disappointed sigh. Celeste is still totally focused on Reed. Except for the dethroning of Krista, the world of the A-list girls is still intact. Nothing's going to change tonight. No magic wand or surprise prince will turn you into Cinderella. You might as well go home.

You go back through the concession and rental room, take off your skates, and get your coat. You call a cab from the pay phone, and step outside into the dark. A fine, cold, wet mist floats down through the outdoor lights. Your breath comes out in a damp cloud of white. Someone is standing in a shadow to your right, staying under an overhang to keep out of the drizzle. This person sees you, too, and backs deeper into the shadow as if not wanting to be recognized. But it's too late. You know it's Krista. She must be waiting for a ride, too.

Here you both stand, separated by the cold mist that glitters in the light. How strange. In a way you're both leaving the skating party for the same reason—because of Celeste. Can you go over and talk to Krista? Why can't she come over and talk to you?

It's odd, but you feel bad for her. Maybe because you also know how it feels to be tricked and used. But could you say that to her? Would she ever admit it? Maybe she's not in the mood to talk. Maybe you're not either.

She steps out of the shadow and looks straight at you. "Do you need a ride, Lauren?"

Caught by surprise, you hardly know what to say. "It's . . . in the other direction."

Krista smiles ever so slightly. Ever so sadly. "I know where you live, silly."

And she does, of course, because she used to live across the street.

"I'm kind of waiting for a cab," you explain.

Krista pulls a small black phone out of her bag. "I can tell them not to come."

"Well, then sure, thanks. That's really nice of you."

Krista calls the taxi company and informs them that you no longer need the cab. You cannot help being a little in awe of how mature and confident she sounds when speaking to that unseen grown-up at the cab company switchboard. Then she turns off the phone and drops it back into her bag. Once again you look at each other. The wet mist is cool and chilly against your face. It collects on the roof and drips off the eaves to the ground.

"Remember weeks ago you told me to be careful with Celeste?" you ask. "That something wasn't right with her? How did you know?"

Krista shrugs. "It was just a feeling."

"Then why were you friendly to her?"

The soft lines around Krista's mouth deepen slightly. As if the answer is painfully obvious. "I had no choice."

"I . . . I don't get it," you admit.

"Celeste was going to be popular whether I liked it or not. Everyone knew it the second they saw her."

"So you had to be her friend?" you realize.

The little smile on Krista's lips is wrinkled and bitter, like a crabapple. "Stupid, isn't it?"

A large dark car coated with a dull film of moisture pulls up and Krista steps completely out of the shadow. You also start toward the car. Just then, someone behind you says, "Lauren?"

You turn to find Rob standing in the doorway of the skating rink, backlit by the lights from inside. His hands jammed into his pockets, he asks, "You're not going home, are you?"

You don't know how to answer.

"I, uh, thought maybe you'd like to stay and do something," he says.

You look back at Krista, waiting by the car. Won't she be angry? But she smiles. "What are you waiting for? Go, girl."

"But . . ."

Krista waves at you. "We'll talk, okay? Later." She gets into the car and pulls the door closed.

You turn back toward Rob. "That's a really nice-looking outfit, Lauren."

"Thank you, Rob." Maybe something *has* changed after all.

chapter
twenty-eight

Back inside, Rob waits while you hang up your coat again. "So, want to play some video games?"

"Why don't we skate?" you ask.

"Uh, because I'm the worst skater ever?" He grins.

"Worse than me at video games?" You grin back.

"How about, first we play some video games, then we skate?"

"Sounds like a plan."

You prove to be as bad at video games as you promised, and it's not long before Rob agrees to go skating.

"You weren't that bad for a beginner," he says while he laces up his scuffed black rental skates.

"Then how come I used up four times as many tokens as you?" you ask.

"Don't worry, it will all even out on the ice."

You soon see that Rob wasn't joking about not being a good skater. He might be even worse than Celeste. Once you're on the ice, it's not a question of trying to hold him up. He clings to the rail and refuses to let go.

"You won't learn to skate if you don't let go," you tell him.

"I won't learn if I do let go," he answers. "All I'll do is learn to fall."

"What are you afraid of?" You laugh.

"How about breaking every bone in my body?"

"I've fallen a million times. It doesn't hurt as much as you think."

"Yeah, right." Rob rolls his eyes as if to let you know he thinks you're certifiably insane.

In one of the boldest moves you've ever made, you slide your arm through his. "Okay, look. I promise one of two things will happen. Either you won't fall, or I'll fall with you."

Rob finally lets go and you help him around the rink. His skates keep slipping out from under him and you almost do fall several times. But at least it's late and most of the kids have stopped skating. Few are around to witness what clods you are together. Each time the double doors swing open, you catch a glimpse of Celeste, Reed, Shelby, and Jason in the snack bar. It makes you feel bad.

So you try not to look.

Finally, Rob actually does begin to skate a little.

And you forget to look.

Then the skating rink lights blink on and off and a voice on the loudspeaker announces that the rink is closing for the night. You realize that you and Rob are just about the only ones left on the ice.

"Aw, darn," Rob complains. "I was just getting ready to do a triple axel into a quadruple toeloop."

"Guess you'll just have to wait until next time."

He grins. "That was fun, Lauren. Thanks for teaching me."

"No prob."

You leave the ice together. And clop on your skates into the snack bar/rental area. Hardly anyone's around. Celeste and the others are gone. The music has been turned off. It's quiet. In the snack bar they're scraping the grill and washing out the fryers.

You and Rob quietly untie your skates. "Guess it really is time to go," Rob says after he returns his skates to the rental counter. "You need a ride?"

"Okay, thanks."

Rob calls his parents and a little while later Mr. Carlucci arrives. You and Rob sit together in the back. Mr. Carlucci asks if you had fun and you both say yes, but aside from that, most of the ride home is quiet. At your house, Rob hops out and holds the door open for you. You step out into the night. The neighborhood is quiet. The houses are dark and the air is chilly. The street is still glistening wet, but the mist has passed, and between the dark shadows of clouds the sky is filled with twinkling stars. Rob walks with you to your front door and you actually feel nervous that he may try to kiss you. But he wouldn't with his father watching from the car, would he?

"That was fun," he says, standing near you while you unlock your front door.

"Yes."

He shoves his hands into his pockets. "So, uh, see you in school Monday?"

"Where else?"

"Yeah." He shrugs. "Guess you're right."

You get the door open and turn to him. "Thanks, Rob." And then, in an impulse that comes from you don't know where, you lean forward and kiss him on the cheek.

twenty-nine

"You must have gotten in awful late last night, hon."

"Pretty late."

"Have fun?" (Why must every adult ask this? you wonder.)

"Of course."

And it's strange because it was both the best and worst night of your life, and you're still really not sure how you feel. Rob is nice, and he's the first boy who's ever really paid any attention to you. But every time you think of Celeste, you feel like crying.

The weekend passes slowly. You do homework, watch TV, and baby-sit. Hardly a minute passes that you don't think of picking up the phone and calling Celeste. You want to ask her why she led you along, why she lied to you. Why'd she even bother with you?

You are proud that you manage not to call her. What would be the point? No matter what she said you probably wouldn't believe her. The few times the phone rings, you let your mom answer it. You're slightly afraid it will be Celeste with a new story, a new explanation, a new lie.

"Hon, it's for you," Mom says around eight o'clock on Sunday night after she answers the phone.

"Who is it?" you ask warily.

"A boy."

You pick up. "Hello?"

"Hi." It's Rob. "So what's up?"

"Just doing homework. You?"

"Same." And it's obvious that he really has no reason for calling. Except to talk.

chapter
thirty

At school on Monday morning, you don't even look for Celeste in the hall. It's strange, but you feel a different kind of confidence. The confidence not to need her anymore.

You've barely gotten seated in Spanish class when you're called down to the office. You can't imagine what the problem is this time. After all, you've already paid for the skating party. As you reach the office, you're surprised to find Celeste coming out and into the hallway. That's strange because you didn't hear any announcement calling her down to see the principal.

Neither of you smiles or says anything about the skating party.

"What's going on?" you ask.

Celeste tips her head down and her eyes practically vanish behind her bangs. "You better go in. There's still some kind of problem."

For a moment neither of you moves. You just look at each other. You're dying to tell her that she's a liar and a phony, but you know it won't change anything. Besides, you never say things like that. You're always too scared. You'll just stand there and let Celeste think she's won Reed for herself and taken over Queen Krista's throne. You doubt anyone will ever be able to sink her ship.

Celeste turns to go, but as she does, you feel your lips begin to move as if they have a mind of their own. "Have fun at the skating party?"

Celeste stops and slowly turns back to you. She parts her bangs with a finger and her eyes narrow. You catch a glimpse of something you never saw in her before. Something fierce and determined. Something that knows it must fight and win to survive. "You wouldn't understand."

"I think I might."

Then, unexpectedly, Celeste's lips twist into a hard little smile. "You'd better go in. Principal Hansen is waiting."

In her office Principal Hansen has a stern look on her face. The eyebrows dip. She taps the eraser end of a black pencil against a manila folder on her desk. "Have a seat, Lauren."

You feel a deep and uncomfortable chill. Goose bumps rise on your skin and your heart begins to bang. Either the air just became really heavy or you're suddenly having trouble breathing. Principal Hansen opens the manila folder. Inside are photocopies of deposit and withdrawal slips.

"I have some very disturbing news, Lauren," she says. "It appears that on the same day the class account was closed, you opened a bank account and deposited a large amount of money."

It takes a moment to understand what she is implying. "But . . . that was my money."

"What does that mean to you?" Principal Hansen asks.

"It means I earned it. Every penny. It took almost two years."

"How?"

"Baby-sitting."

Principal Hansen slides one of the sheets of paper toward you. "Then why did you withdraw the money from your account and use it to pay for the skating party?"

You stare down at the sheet of paper. It's a photocopy of the withdrawal slip you filled out to get the money for the party.

"Because the party was going to be canceled if I didn't," you explain.

"Why would you use your hard-earned money for that?" Principal Hansen asks. "It was just a class party."

You stare at her dumfounded. How can you explain what that party was supposed to mean? What Celeste promised it would mean? Now Principal Hansen slides a second sheet of paper toward you.

"Do you recognize this?" she asks.

It's a photocopy of a withdrawal slip taking $517 out of the class bank account. There are two signatures on it. Yours and Celeste's.

"I . . . I never saw this before in my life."

Principal Hansen places the two sheets of paper next to each other. "Look at the two withdrawal slips. Your signature is almost identical on both. Now look at Celeste's signature on the withdrawal slip and this copy of her signature that I just asked her to sign."

Principal Hansen slides a third piece of paper toward me. On it is Celeste's signature.

"Celeste Van Warner was just here," Principal Hansen explains. "I asked her to sign her name on this piece of paper. If you compare this signature to the signature on the withdrawal slip, does it look familiar?

The two signatures look vaguely similar. But the one on the withdrawal slip is rougher, as if a child scrawled it.

You look up and straight into Principal Hansen's eyes.

"Do you want to change your story?" she asks.

"Absolutely not. I never saw that withdrawal slip before in my life. Whoever did it must have forged my signature."

Principal Hansen presses her lips together and looks disappointed. It's obvious that she doesn't believe you.

"On each withdrawal slip *your* signature looks very similar," she says. "The only signature that looks forged is Celeste's."

Your stomach tightens and you start to feel sick. Everything has been turned inside out. If anything, you thought you would have been a hero for replacing the missing class money with your own. Instead you're being accused of stealing the money in the first place!

"Celeste just told me that you came to her and admitted that you took the skating money," Principal Hansen says.

You feel your jaw go slack and your whole body go weak. As if every drop of blood just drained out. "That's not true . . ." Your voice cracks and comes out like a whimper.

"Celeste says she encouraged you to take the money out of your account and use it to pay for the skating party."

"No," you whisper.

Principal Hansen points at the deposit and withdrawal slips. "Then how do you explain this?"

You remember the afternoon Celeste came to your house and put makeup on you, and how much fun you had . . . and how she insisted on practicing signatures. Even then she had it all planned. You gaze across the desk at your principal. "You'd never believe me."

Principal Hansen leans back in her chair and stares at you. Having done nothing to be ashamed about, you look right back at her. But you can feel tears welling up and spilling out of your eyes. Only they're stupid tears. Tears that spring up for the wrong reason.

Principal Hansen lets out a long, deep breath. "Maybe I won't believe you, but I want you to tell me."

So you tell her the whole story. How Celeste became your friend and made you feel better about yourself than you ever imagined you could feel. How thanks to her you did things you never thought you'd do, wore clothes you never thought you'd wear, and made friends you never thought you'd make. How you gained the confidence to do things you never dreamed you'd do. Like speaking your mind and admitting when you'd made a mistake. How you truly don't know what happened to the class's money, but you're not sorry you used yours to pay for the skating party. Because even though it didn't turn out the way you'd wanted, you learned something important and had a good time anyway.

Principal Hansen taps her pencil against the desk and looks over the papers. "The skating party cost three hundred dollars. Five hundred and seventeen was taken out of the class account."

More than enough for a pretty pink skating outfit, you think ruefully, blotting the tears out of your eyes and feeling them get dry again. Despite everything you feel good inside. You've done nothing wrong. "I don't know what happened to it," you reply. "I never saw or touched any of that money. Not one penny."

Once again, Principal Hansen gazes at you. This time for quite a while. Her lips part. She hesitates, then says, "You'll have to resign as co-treasurer."

You don't want that job anymore anyway. "Okay."

Principal Hansen frowns. "All right, Lauren. You can go."

thirty-one

At lunch you sit with Tara in the land of the socially inferior. Over toward the middle of the cafeteria Celeste now sits at the center of the DYWYWM table. She is clearly the new queen. Judy Knight sits on one side of her, and Shelby Kirk sits on the other. Even Stephanie Eisley is there, still clinging to her wanna-be spot near the end of the table.

Krista isn't in the cafeteria. You wonder if she is hiding at home with a pretend stomachache. Or maybe she has exiled herself to the library. Maybe that's what you should have done, too. Since your meeting this morning with Principal Hansen your emotions have been all over the place. A graph of them would look like a major earthquake on the Richter scale, or the jagged edges of a broken window. Spikes going high when you've felt good because you know inside you've done nothing wrong. Then deep valleys of despair when you catch someone in class giving you a curious look. You're fairly certain they're wondering if you're really a thief. The story of the stolen class funds, or various forms of it, has spread all over school. It isn't hard to guess who's been spreading it.

And now, here in the crowded cafeteria, you feel lower than ever. The kids glance from their tables at you. You stare down at your oily tuna sandwich. You chose not to buy lunch today just because you didn't want anyone to think you were buying it with class money. You have less than no appetite. They must all despise and hate you. What could possibly be lower than stealing school money? Maybe you could convince your mom to send you to the parochial school in town. Or would the story just follow you there, too?

"What's wrong?" Tara says.

"Do you have to ask?" you moan. "I feel like killing myself."

"Hold it," Tara says. "You're only supposed to say that if you've done something wrong. Not if you're innocent."

"How do you know I'm innocent?" you ask.

"Oh, give me a break, Lauren," Tara snorts. "I'm your friend, dummy. You'd never do something like that."

"But *they* don't know that." You tilt your head at the rest of the cafeteria.

"Who cares about them?" Tara asks.

"I do."

"Well, you shouldn't."

You give her a sad look. Maybe you shouldn't care, but you do. It's something Tara will never understand. It's something you're not even sure *you* understand. You just know it's a lot more important to you than it is to her.

But that doesn't stop Tara from trying to cheer you up. "Come on, Lauren, how long have we known each other? Since second grade? You're the most honest person I know. And, no offense, but you couldn't have come up with a plan like that in a million years."

"Thanks." You give her a crooked smile.

"I *told* you I didn't trust that girl." Tara chews pensively on her jerky. "I knew there was something bad about her. I could see it."

"How come I couldn't?" you ask.

"You could've if you'd wanted to. You just didn't want to."

Tara's right, but what difference does it make now?

chapter
thirty-two

Rob comes out of the lunch line with a tray. He swivels his head to the right and then left, as if looking for someone to sit with. You quickly look down again and feel your face begin to burn. Now that this story about you taking the class money is going around, you might as well forget about him, too. You really have to hand it to Celeste. She not only knew how to get what she wanted. She knew how to make sure she was the *only* one who got it. Severely cold-blooded.

"What a day, huh?"

You look up into Rob's face as he puts his tray down and sits across from you. This is a total shock. And what does he mean? Did something else happen today that you haven't heard about?

"You believe that Lauren took that money?" Tara asks.

"Tara!" you gasp, and feel your face instantly grow flushed.

"Let him answer," Tara says.

Rob shakes his head. "Not a chance."

Tara turns to you. "See, Lauren? Your *real* friends know the truth."

You look at Rob, not knowing what to say. He looks back at you. "It's one of those stories that sounds really juicy until you stop and think about it. Then you realize it doesn't make any sense."

You feel your eyes begin to get watery, but this time you manage to blink back the tears. "Thanks, Rob."

Someone else slides down the table and sits next to you. It's . . . Krista?

"I just talked to Principal Hansen," she announces. "She told me about your resigning as class treasurer. I said no way. If you resign, I resign."

"Hey, me, too," adds Rob.

You're totally stunned. Like, in shock. "Why?" you finally manage to croak.

"Oh, come on, Lauren," Krista goes, like its completely obvious. "I know you. We *grew* up together."

thirty-three

You wish you could report that Celeste got caught or punished or hit by a car. But nothing bad has happened to her. She still sits every day at the DYWYWM table with Shelby, and Stephanie and the others. She did resign as class treasurer, saying that she did so because she couldn't get along with Krista. And Principal Hansen did reinstate you to the position after Krista, Rob, and Judy all said that's what they wanted.

You still sit with Tara at your table at the edge of the cafeteria. Sometimes Rob sits with you. Sometimes he sits with some other boys. Sometimes Krista and Judy sit with you. Sometimes they don't.

In a strange way, what Celeste predicted has partly come true. The popular crowd has broken up. The A-list girls have spread out. Celeste reigns over the old DYWYWM table, but there are days now when that table is half empty and there is elbowroom to spare.

One morning in the hall before homeroom, you saw

Celeste at the locker of a girl named Robin Jeffers. Robin is tall and gawky, with long brown hair that she always parts in the middle. She's quiet and has only one or two friends, and most kids would never suspect that she is a musical genius on the cello. You watched as Robin slid a homework sheet out of her notebook and gave it to Celeste. Then Celeste put her hand on Robin's shoulder and spoke softly and meaningfully. You caught the yearning, envious look in Robin's eyes as she watched Celeste go off down the hall.

If you knew Robin better, perhaps you could go over and say something. Instead you will keep an eye on her. It may not be any of your business. Maybe it would be better to let Robin learn the same lesson you learned. But you don't think you can allow that to happen. You're not that kind of person. And that's good.

Once in a while you still feel like crying. Because Celeste deceived you and used you. And because you let her do it.

But more often now you're pretty happy. You wear makeup when you feel like it. And the other day you came to school in the slinkiest pink tank top your crazy aunt Sarah from California sent. When Shelby and Stephanie saw you, they whispered to each other. And you just smiled because it didn't bother you at all. They're not your friends and you don't care what they think. You just feel lucky that you do have a few good real friends. You care about them and you know they care about you. It's something you feel confident about. And that is what's truly important.